THE PRINCESS TROLL

THE SEATTLE TROLLS TRILOGY: BOOK TWO

LEAH R CUTTER

BOOK VIEW CAFE

Come someplace new…
If you'd like to be notified of new releases, sign up for my newsletter.

I will never spam you or use your email for nefarious purposes. You can also unsubscribe at any time.

http://www.LeahCutter.com/newsletter/

The Clockwork Fairy Kingdom

The Clockwork Fairy Kingdom

The Maker, the Teacher, and the Monster

The Dwarven Wars

The Chronicles of Franklin

Franklin Versus The Popcorn Thief

Franklin Versus The Soul Thief

Franklin Versus The Child Thief

Contemporary Fantasy

Siren's Call

The Immortals' War

Circle of Air

CHAPTER 1

"Try it again," Nikolai told Christine.

With a huge, trollish sigh, Christine focused on her hand again. It shouldn't be so hard to create a flame in the palm of her hand. She was supposedly a magical creature, a troll capable of doing magic, one of the few. And possibly trollish royalty…though that wasn't something she dwelt on.

It was easy enough for Christine to generate a constant illusion around herself so she appeared human, with dark, olive-toned skin, human hair and eyes. For her to camouflage her green troll skin (tough and strong), the large tusks growing up out of her lower jaw to just below her cheekbones (which she'd finally gotten used to eating with), and her claws, which always seemed to nick and tear anything she picked up if she wasn't careful (as evidenced by her poor cell phone). To change her clothes with her appearance, so her blouse always went with whatever color her skin was (so even now she looked good in a cream-colored top), her pants showing off her curves (stretchy and black, currently), shoes appearing and disappearing (the claws on her feet couldn't be contained).

Magical powders and other charms reacted to her presence, boiling over or glowing, so she had no doubt that she was magical.

However, in the past six months since learning she was a changeling, and was actually a troll and not a human, she hadn't been able to consciously learn any magic.

Christine focused all of her will on her trollish palm, the skin there surprisingly pink compared to the tough, green-colored hide that covered the rest of her. While the nail beds were still pinkish, the nails themselves were solid white, naturally pointed like claws, and sharp. She'd tried using an emery board on them. Once. Had shredded it to bits.

"I don't know what's wrong," Nikolai said. The wooden shopkeeper scowled at her hand, as if it had insulted him.

Christine was always impressed with how expressive Nik's wooden face was, despite how his black, round eyes were painted on. His lips had also merely been drawn on, going in a straight line, but he could make all the sounds she could without ever changing the shape of his mouth, just opening and closing it on hinges. It was like watching a live ventriloquist's doll, except not as creepy.

He wore his usual Seattle-chic red-and-white checked flannel shirt and jeans. Even in his black boots he only stood about three feet high. He barely reached Christine's waist. In her human form, she was close to six feet. As a troll, she was only a touch taller.

The pair of them stood in a supply room at the back of

Nikolai's Magical Emporium. The shop itself existed between worlds. The only way to get to it was through a magical portal. Christine traveled there using the portal located in Seattle's International District. She often wondered if she could leave the shop through a different portal, ending up in one of the pocket worlds.

Dark red-velvet curtains closed the supply room off from the rest of the shop. Tall metal shelves filled with plain brown cardboard boxes rose from floor to ceiling. It looked like an ordinary storeroom, except for the glowing, neon-blue stickers on the boxes of conductive powder, the way the crystals in their box rustled, and the slightly sweet scent of burnt sugar and marjoram and something *else* that was pure magic.

The light in the back room was bright and cheery, like the lights in the rest of the store. Christine now knew that what looked like ordinary fluorescent lights hanging from the ceiling of the shop were actually enspelled: Each customer perceived the light in the manner they found most appealing, making the shop seem gloomy, or dappled in moonlight, or even daylight bright.

Christine hadn't realized she liked bright and cheery. That generally wasn't her thing. Nikolai had assured her that it probably wasn't the light she wanted to live by, just to shop by. And that made sense.

Nikolai was all about being inclusive. He didn't turn away any customers, not *kith and kin*—Christine's people, the orcs, trolls, goblins, dwarves, brownies, and so on— nor the Host either. All of the ranks of demons and angels were welcome in his shop. He'd even serve the occasional human wizard, though rarely: Humans had their own stores that they preferred going to.

However, Nikolai's Magical Emporium was neutral territory, and Nik worked hard to keep it that way.

Once Christine had realized that she was magical, the shopkeeper had offered to help her learn spells.

Of course, he wouldn't do it for free. He was too much of a businessman for that.

Since Christine could barely afford the ingredients for spells, let alone the lessons, Nikolai had bartered for her skills instead. So now, every other weekend, Christine put in some hours at the shop. Not out front, working with customers. She was a troll, after all. Dealing with people wasn't her forte.

For her human day job she worked as an archivist in the main Seattle library. She was good with research papers and books. She paid for her magic lessons by going through the huge collection of boxes Nikolai had accumulated at estate sales over the years, finding the important documents, treaties, and books hidden away amidst all the junk and developing a filing system for them.

While Nikolai now had an impressive inventory for all his hidden treasures, the magic lessons hadn't gone according to plan at all. Christine could still barely do any magic.

Christine stared at her palm, willing a light to grow there, forcing her hand to stay steady and not shake in frustration. She took a deep breath, scenting the comforting smells of old papers and long forgotten books. She just needed to focus.

Tina, Christine's human doppelganger, was extremely talented magically. She'd also been trying to teach Christine some magic, with the same awful results as Nikolai had achieved.

Tina *glowed* when she even thought about doing serious magic. She hadn't left any scorch marks (yet) on Christine's rug. But she sometimes grew so bright she hurt Christine's eyes.

Christine couldn't even cheat and start with a match to get some magical light.

"I think," Nikolai said when Christine dropped her palm, frustrated as always at her lack of success, "that something's blocking you."

"What do you mean?" Christine asked. She didn't mean to bristle at him. It was just her trollish nature.

"You were hidden for years by the changeling spell," Nikolai said, reaching up to stroke his smooth wooden jaw as if it had suddenly sprouted a beard. "You weren't allowed to be yourself. Maybe that's still affecting you."

Christine nodded slowly. That almost made sense. The changeling spell had made Christine not only look like a human, but act like a human as well.

The changeling spell had been broken when Christine and Tina had met for the first time. Irresistibly drawn to one another, they'd touched hands.

Both of their worlds had imploded.

However, it didn't feel to Christine as though the changeling spell was still holding her back. She didn't think there were any remnants of it remaining.

Then again, what did she know about magic?

"I can ask Tina," Christine said.

Nikolai made a sour face at that. Fascinating how his cheeks gave the impression of moving without actually moving, how his lips appeared to pucker. "Never trust a human," he told her, as he frequently did.

"I know," Christine said, nodding. "But I'm not sure who else to ask." While she could ask Joe, her on-again, off-again boyfriend and the only other troll she knew, he wouldn't be able to tell her anything. He didn't have any magic, and any talk of her magic always made him uncomfortable.

Besides, they were on a "break" right now. Not seeing other people, but not seeing so much of each other either.

Christine had been fascinated with how her body responded as a troll, but it had been…too much. Everything had been too new. She'd been overwhelmed quickly both by her feelings and her responses to him.

She didn't know any other trolls, either. There weren't many in Seattle as far as she could tell. Trolls were solitary in nature, something she did know very well. They didn't tend to get together for drinks or join the other *kith and kin*.

Nikolai gave her a sharp nod. "Then ask your Tina. But take anything she says with a mountain of salt."

"I will," Christine promised. She knew that Nikolai would never trust any human. Not even Christine's human brother Dennis, though he was probably the human that Nikolai was nicest to.

Christine always felt as if she could trust Tina. Her human doppelganger had tried to help Christine fit into the human world once she'd discovered she was a troll and her true nature had come to the forefront.

However, Tina's parents, Mr. and Mrs. Zimmerman, were another matter entirely.

They'd officially "adopted" Christine from her bio-parents, through an agency that no longer existed. But they hadn't kept her or raised her. Instead, they'd performed spells on Christine so that she'd look just like Tina. To be Tina's identical twin.

Then they'd exchanged Tina and Christine at birth.

The switch had fooled the demons, so they'd kept an eye on Christine while Tina grew powerfully magical out of sight. So Tina could fulfill her Destiny.

Christine didn't trust Tina's parents as far as she could throw them, and in her troll body, she could heave them quite a ways. Possibly halfway across Lake Union.

"Come by half an hour earlier tomorrow," Nikolai told Christine.

Christine merely nodded. She could tell by Nikolai's eyes—maybe it was the way they shone—that he had something up his red-and-white flannel sleeve. She also knew he wouldn't say a thing until that time.

She reached up to her neck with one hand and touched her illusion charm, a lovely dark blue stone encased in a swirling silver setting, then held out her other hand so she could watch herself change. Watch the pink skin roll up under the green (her human self was smaller and less muscular than her troll self). Watch the soft, downy, human hair sprout over her arms. Watch the change roll across her chest, her clothes changing with it, until she was wearing a tight peach blouse that contrasted beautifully with her olive skin, plain jeans, and white sneakers.

Christine didn't need the charm she wore around her neck to change her appearance. It was one of the few magical spells that she could actually do, and do consistently. However, the charm was a good reminder to her that she needed to stay human, act human, and not *troll out* as her brother Dennis teased her.

Why was changing herself so easy, while changing anything else so difficult? Dennis would say it was because she was inherently resistant to change. She *hated* change, actually. Had lived in the same apartment for years. Had the same job. The same routine.

Magic was different, though. Magic was something she was supposed to be able to do, had always *longed* to do. Had read far too many books about, both before and after she'd found out about being a troll.

It wasn't all in her head, Christine knew. Something was blocking her.

But what?

~

Christine hadn't bothered going to church with her parents for years, even though they still asked her to go with them every Sunday.

She felt even more uncomfortable going now. It wasn't like she was a demon or something, but churches were for humans.

And Christine really was no longer human.

She didn't go to the services that the *kith and kin* held up in Fremont either, under the Aurora bridge, where the giant statue of a troll lay, holding an actual VW bug in one hand.

She wasn't sure what she believed, now that she knew that both demons and angels were real.

Did that mean that God and Satan were real too? And how did she feel about that? Or was the Host actually made up of creatures like herself, magical, non-human beings who just claimed to be on one side or the other?

She'd seen angels, though she'd never actually talked with one. She had met and talked with demons. She didn't like them one bit, though the *kith and kin* were more often allied with demons than with humans.

So while Mum and Dad were at church that Sunday morning, Christine went to her own place of worship: the huge used bookstore downtown. Here was where she communed with old friends, Jane Austin and Karen Joy Fowler, Judith Tarr and Walter Tervin. So many new friends to find among the towering shelves. The wonderful scent of paper and ink. The soft murmuring of the other worshipers also reverently perusing the stacks, bowing their heads to each other passing through the narrow aisles, like monks greeting each other.

One of the reasons Christine loved this store was because they shelved the used books right next to the new ones. That way, she could often find the start of a series, the used books shelved alongside the latest volume.

Though Christine was living a life of fantasy and knew that magic was real (even if she couldn't do much of it herself) she still felt the need for a good escape now and again, worlds she could delve into and forget herself.

While many people had abandoned paper books for

ebooks, Christine still loved the feel of a book in her hands, the weight of it as she held it open, the slickness of the cover under her fingers. Was it because she was actually a troll? Her brother had always accused her of hording her books. Sure, there were only small aisles between the piles of books in her basement apartment.

Okay, so the books might have covered all the available spaces in every room.

There were worse habits she could have, worse things she could collect. But she couldn't stand cats, or dogs, or most animals, really.

So Christine spent the time before she had to go to her parents for Sunday dinner at the bookstore, perusing, reading a bit here and there, letting the words sing to her soul as she girded her loins.

It wasn't that her parents were bad people. They weren't.

There were days, though, when she'd rather fight an entire demon army than break bread with them.

~

"Any news from Joe?" Mum asked as she passed the garlic mashed potatoes to her right.

They all sat around the dining room table, Mum, Dad, Dennis, and Christine.

Christine sighed. She never should have mentioned him to her parents, her on-again, off-again, troll boyfriend. "We're on a break," she told Mum defensively.

"Sorry to hear that," Dennis said, interrupting any of Mum's questions. "He seemed like a good guy."

"He is," Christine said.

But she wasn't ready. Before, when she'd thought of herself as human, she'd thought she'd never be ready.

Now, she knew that she would be. Eventually.

Just not yet.

Afternoon sunlight gleamed on Lake Washington. The tall glass doors leading to the porch were closed, unfortunately—it had been wickedly hot all summer, and that Sunday was no exception. Fortunately, Mum and Dad's place had air conditioning, unlike most Seattle homes.

Discreet artwork hung on the walls, tiny old-fashioned black-and-white photographs of Mum's family in England, of Dad's family here in Seattle. Though Dad had his own office, he'd also taken over a desk in the dining room, covering it with model airplanes he built out of balsa wood. Christine could still smell the acrid scent of the glue he'd used. A half-finished plane sat on the desk, bright red and blue paint across the bi-wings, while the fuselage was still plain wood.

Thick brown rugs covered the golden hardwood floor. Mum couldn't grow any plants and the tall sticks—the remains of what had been bamboo trees—stood in pots on either side of the door.

Christine sat facing her mum and the water. It didn't matter where she sat. She still would have been uncomfortable. She preferred her underground apartment with its dim lights and comforting mess, snug and cozy.

This house, as well as the new place Dennis had just bought, was far too open and light. Tina would have loved them both, but she was all about light and air.

Dennis asked Dad about something he'd read in the news, a company that was splitting itself into a myriad of companies, and they were off, discussing the pros and cons of such diversification.

Christine didn't try to follow their conversation but concentrated on the food instead. At least Mum had actually listened to her and no longer tried to force bread on her. Meat and veggies were the only things that tasted good to Christine anymore. She wasn't exactly sure why. She used to like bread. Now, it tasted like cardboard, even the fresh artesian rolls she used to get at the health food store.

Only after there were a few moments of silence did Christine look up from her plate. Mum had outdone herself with her good pot roast, the meat perfectly salted and tender, with a tomato sauce and carrots. "Excuse me?" Christine managed to ask as she swallowed down her forkful.

Since the changeling spell had broken, she'd needed to eat more than her human self. It was expensive, but she was figuring out how best to cook for herself, to get the most out of the toughest (and cheapest) cuts of meat she could buy.

"I asked how the magic lessons were going," Mum said quietly.

Christine swallowed again, her mouth suddenly dry. Mum had on her brave face, the one she wore when she asked about her much-changed daughter.

On the one hand, Christine knew her mum actually was curious about her new troll life. On the other, it grated on Mum how different her daughter was now, how little they could relate to each other.

Christine wanted to lie to her family, to tell them that the magic lessons were going well, that she was learning everything quickly now.

However, she'd made the decision early on not to hide from her human family. There were too many others, strangers and acquaintances and co-workers who could never know the truth.

She had to trust someone. She figured her family, the ones who had raised her and had loved her despite her many differences, was a good place to start.

"Not good," Christine admitted. "Nikolai thinks that maybe the changeling spell is blocking me still." Christine didn't agree, but she wanted to tell her parents something. Anything. Because she was blocked, just not by that spell.

"Is there anything we can do to help?" Dad asked. "I'd be happy to build you something to practice on, if that's something you need."

"Thanks, Dad," Christine said. It meant a lot to her that her family was trying to be supportive, even if they didn't quite know what that meant. She didn't know what to suggest to them either.

"Sis," Dennis said, then he paused. "Have you thought about maybe practicing magic someplace other than here?"

"Not in Seattle?" Christine asked. "Like, out in Bellevue?"

"No," Dennis said. "You remember how Ty took us to a different world? I think he called it a pocket world?

Maybe you should try learning magic in one of those places. They're probably more magical to begin with."

Christine nodded slowly. "That's a really good idea, actually," she told Dennis. When Tina had been stolen by demons, Ty Brooks—a professional demon hunter—had followed the trail the demons had left to a different world, bringing both Christine and Dennis with him.

She didn't know if Ty would just take her someplace else. He only traveled between worlds when he was hunting something.

It wouldn't hurt to ask, though, when she saw him next week.

~

Christine let herself into Nikolai's shop thirty minutes before her normal late-afternoon shift. The shop was empty of customers, which was good.

She always loved it here, though she was still trying to get Nikolai to expand the books section. Colorful advertisements covered the walls, written mostly in orcish, elvish, Hebrew, and Sanskrit. The ads were for every type of magical thing imaginable. Blue velvet bags full of glowing gems. Charms of protection and defense. Magical ribbons to bind things together. Silver scissors for cutting them apart.

The ceilings in the shop were tall, shooting up eighteen feet. Shelves filled the room, most barely reaching Christine's chest. That way Nikolai could reach the items on the top shelf without having to get a ladder.

The shop was empty, but Christine didn't bother

calling out. Nik knew she was here. She wasn't sure if it was a spell he had, or some sort of magical sense that always told him when a customer had arrived.

In the six months that she'd worked part-time at the shop, she'd never met another wooden man. Was he the only one? A constructed being? Kind of like Pinocchio? Except he looked like a man and not a boy. He'd been alive for an awfully long time—more than two thousand years, if his stories were to be believed. And he'd been a shopkeeper the entire time. Though he hadn't always had his own store.

Christine walked past the shelves slowly. Nik needed to restock the magical socks the brown men wore—they were enspelled to keep their feet dry, even when covered with bog mud. At the far end of the shop, Christine walked around the counter and slipped behind the blue velvet curtain that hid the storeroom from sight.

Nikolai was already there, wearing a green-and-white flannel shirt today, standing in front of a huge pile of dirt, at least three feet tall and the same around.

The smell of the earth filled Christine's senses. It was moist and fertile. Unlike her mum, Christine could grow anything, though she usually didn't bother with plants in her apartment. The few times she'd tried she'd ended up giving the plants away as they'd quickly gotten out of hand, despite how little sunshine they'd received.

The pile looked completely out of place among the shelves of boxes, lit by the cheery lights, a dark mound on the red carpet. Normally, that sort of thing bothered Christine. She liked things well-ordered, though not necessarily tidy. She knew where every title was in her piles of books at her place. It was a methodical mess.

But the dirt didn't bother her.

"It occurred to me that we were going about this the wrong way," Nikolai said conversationally. "You are, by nature, a creature of the earth. Instead of trying to create something in the air, let's work with the earth instead."

Excitement spiked through Christine. That made total sense! She preferred to be underground. She'd had odd daydreams about warrens and passageways leading off from her basement apartment, tunneling under the earth. They'd be carved out of rock, with beautiful gems still *in situ* in the walls. Rambling and curved, unlike the straight hallways above. Not like a rabbit warren or a hobbit hole. But someplace magical and just hers.

She stepped closer to the pile of dirt eagerly. "What should I do?" she asked.

"I must admit, we've moved beyond my knowledge," Nikolai said. "There aren't many trolls who can do magic, and they've never even been written about, at least as far as I can tell. There are very few stories, even, of troll magic."

Christine nodded, her enthusiasm dimmed but not extinguished. She'd searched as well, looking for troll magic, in every book Nikolai had as well as the internet.

Nothing had fit her or her situation.

"Try to move the pile," Nikolai said. "Or dig in it. Or something."

"Make a tunnel through it?" Christine asked. That was what made the most sense to her.

"Yes! Great," Nikolai said.

Christine considered the pile of dirt. It wasn't big

enough for her to actually dig a proper tunnel through the center of it. But maybe she could create a small one…

She held her hands out in front of her, fingers cupped, as if she were holding grapefruits. They were her troll hands—the presence of the dirt had made her drop her human form without realizing it. She turned her hands to the sides, so her wrists were facing each other. Then she *pushed* from someplace deep inside her, willing an opening to appear in the dirt, a small tunnel, no bigger than the space between her palms.

Christine felt the power leave her. There was a soft *wump* as the magic hit the dirt pile.

However, her only reward was a tiny indentation in the side of the mound.

Christine concentrated harder. She could practically *see* the cone of energy she directed with her hands toward the dirt. It was ghostly and not of this world.

However, Christine couldn't make a tunnel in the dirt. Couldn't make any more of an impression on it.

Maybe the energy she saw was all in her head and it didn't actually exist. Except, she could *feel* it.

Frustrated, Christine snarled. She could do this. She knew she could. This was her birthright. This was something she knew how to do, instinctively. She held her breath and *pushed* with all her will.

She *would* make a tunnel in that earth.

The charm around Christine's neck grew hot as it charged with the excess power she emanated. The air around her sizzled and grew hazy. Even the lights dimmed.

But the dirt refused to budge.

A cool hand suddenly touched Christine's arm. It was

like a switch being thrown. Her power drained into the ether, evaporating quickly. Christine felt herself deflating like a pricked balloon.

"What happened?" Christine asked as she shook her head, trying to clear it.

The dirt pile still stood there, defiantly. A tiny dent dimpled the side, as if a volleyball had lightly bounced off it.

"You have power," Nikolai said slowly. "I could see it."

Christine nodded. She had felt it. It hadn't all just been in her mind.

Nikolai chuckled. "If you'd been able to release it, direct it, you probably would have blown up the entire store."

"Really?" Christine asked. Then she thought back. She had been angry enough to blow apart *something*.

"But," Nikolai said, then paused. "You are being blocked. And not by the changeling spell. There's magic working against you."

"Oh," Christine said. Why would someone do that?

Unless it had to do with her bio-parents.

While the Zimmermans swore that her adoption had been legal, Christine had always had her doubts. The Zimmermans hadn't bothered to keep her but had passed her off almost immediately.

That had to violate the spirit of the adoption, if not the actual letter of it.

But when Christine and Tina had tried to find out who her bio-parents were, the spell had failed. Tina had guessed that the court records had been sealed.

Had her bio-parents given her up for adoption? Even though she was probably of royal blood?

Or had she been stolen? Her natural powers blocked, so she wouldn't be able to…do whatever she was supposed to do?

There was a war going on, after all. The Great War, between the two branches of the Host. The angels and the demons.

Tina was the one who was supposed to have a Destiny, who was supposed to bring an end to the war. Lars, the demon who had masqueraded as Dennis' best friend, had nearly stolen that Destiny from Tina.

Had Christine's Destiny also been taken? Or thwarted? Blocked like her magic?

She didn't know who to ask or where to start looking.

But she was going to get to the bottom of this.

CHAPTER 2

T*y for lunch* had become a running joke between Christine and Ty Brooks, the demon hunter.

That Monday, they really were having Thai food at a little hole in the wall near Christine's library in downtown Seattle. There were four tables in the tiny space beside the industrial counter. The only light came from the large garage door in the front. It wasn't air conditioned, but Christine found she didn't mind the heat as much as she used to. Plus, the floor was concrete and cool in the shade.

Most of the food orders were take-away, so Christine and Ty got a seat immediately, far in the back. The phone kept ringing, more orders pouring in, three different delivery guys collecting the large plastic bags piled on the counter and carting them away to the offices nearby.

The chaos didn't bother Christine as much as it would have before. She was almost getting used to new places, new smells, new food. Before, when Christine had thought she was human, she'd never bothered exploring much or trying new things. She wasn't allergic to new things, no matter how much her brother Dennis might tease her about it. They'd just made her uncomfortable.

For the last six months, she'd made a point of trying new things—new food, new clothes, new books, even new movies. She had no idea what *she* liked, what was *her* and what had come from the spell that had made her identical to Tina. And damn it, she was going to find out.

Her exploration had started when she'd realized that some of her discomfort with trying new things had been a result of being a changeling. The spell that had hidden her had influenced her subtly, making her stay home and not explore. It was meant to keep her safe, to protect her. Limit her.

Which made Christine even more determined to try new things.

Of course, the owner knew Ty. He was a short, bald Asian man in a pristine T-shirt and khaki shorts, wearing flip-flops. He had a face as round as a coconut, with bushy black eyebrows and a ready smile, his nose standing out in sharp relief.

The owner had come over to take their order. They hadn't been to a restaurant or bar yet that Ty wasn't on a first-name basis with at least half the staff. Not every place they'd gone had been strictly human, either.

Christine was starting to get the hang of seeing through illusions, figuring out if a being was human or not. She still struggled with it. Was it because the rest of her power was blocked? She didn't know.

Ty ordered for them. He knew her preferences for meat and veggies, not a lot of noodles or rice. She'd also started eating her food with more spice.

While they waited for their meals, Christine explained what had happened the day before, with Nikolai and the dirt.

Ty gave a low whistle when she finished. "So you got the power, but you can't get at it?" he asked.

Christine nodded morosely. Even Nik hadn't been sure what to do next. There were many ways to bind a being's power. He didn't know enough about how trolls did magic to even take a guess, though he'd volunteered to do some research for her.

Ty was quiet for a moment. He appeared human, a tall, lanky, African American man with a muscled chest and arms. His kind brown eyes looked at her thoughtfully. "Can you describe how it felt, again?" he asked eventually.

"I had the power. Energy. *Something.* It was all in my hands. I just couldn't do anything with it. I could *see* how to focus it, how to shape it into a cone of force. But… nothing. Nothing was actually coming out." Christine made herself take a deep breath. Just thinking about it made her angry.

"It sounds to me like somebody's bound your power," Ty said.

"I keep wondering if it's tied up with my bio-parents. If my power was bound when I was adopted. Or stolen," Christine added darkly.

Ty pursed his lips and thought.

Christine knew better than to interrupt the hunter. He was good at his job, at hunting things. When she'd seen his true self, he appeared to be half-human, half dog. He worked with a whole bunch of machines and chemicals, like some kind of mad scientist, so that he could prove his findings to the court of the Host.

Just finding a demon wasn't always enough in terms of evidence. Sometimes he needed to be able to prove that a demon had been someplace they shouldn't be.

The court gave him most of his jobs, tracking demons that had skipped bail, or were wanted for arrest. Every once in a while he took on a freelance case. He'd never taken Christine with him on a court case—lawyers would claim she'd influenced the results. So he'd only taken Christine hunting with him a couple of times.

"It could be related to how you became a changeling," he said eventually. "The court has sometimes bound a criminal's power so they can't hurt anyone anymore." He snorted. "Course, you can't take away all of a magical being's powers. The only way to do that is to kill them. And we don't live in a capital punishment district."

That was good to know, actually. That no one could take away all of her magic. And that the court wouldn't kill her if she committed some crime.

"So how do I unbind my power?" Christine asked as the owner came back. He slid a pile of stir-fried pork and broccoli in front of Christine, with a small serving of rice on the side, while giving Ty a huge bowl of noodles with chicken and cashews. He also placed two large glasses of Thai iced coffee on the table before heading back to the counter.

Ty ate for a minute while he thought. He used chopsticks deftly. Christine used a fork to try her food. It was tasty, spices that danced on her tongue, solid meat that made her mouth want more, the broccoli still crunchy and then flavored with sesame and coconut oil. And the Thai iced coffee was divine, sweet and cool with just the right amount of coffee flavor.

"You have to bind a person's power *to* something," Ty said eventually. "Generally to something outside of him or her. Like to a rock, or a tree, or something."

"So my power isn't tied up inside of me?" Christine asked, surprised. She'd assumed that her magic was bound up inside her, somehow.

Ty shook his head. "That's how the most magical of enchanted items get made. By binding someone's power to them."

Christine paused for a moment, puzzled. Nikolai knew about that, certainly. He'd been a shopkeeper for a really long time. Why hadn't he mentioned that her power might be tied to an artifact?

Then again, Nik wouldn't say anything until he was one hundred percent certain.

"How do I find this artifact?" Christine asked. "Would I be drawn to it?"

"That would make it too easy for a criminal to find them," Ty replied, shaking his head. "And you wouldn't be repulsed by the thing either. You'd feel neutral about it."

"I'm not a criminal," Christine said hotly. "I didn't commit any crime. Someone committed a crime on me. Or to me."

"Sorry—didn't meant to imply you were," Ty said. "It's just…those are the only cases I know of. When someone's power has been removed." He paused, then continued. "If your power has been bound to some kind of artifact, it's going to be well guarded."

Christine nodded. That made sense. Whoever had taken her magic hadn't done so lightly, and didn't want her to be able to get it back easily.

But who had done it? And why?

"Have you always lived in the same neighborhood?" Ty asked suddenly.

"I was raised in Madison Valley, down the hill, near Lake Washington," Christine said. "But when I started school at Seattle University, I moved to the Central District, and have been there ever since." The neighborhood lines had changed recently, with Central District shrinking. She actually lived in the Capitol Hill neighborhood now, but she refused to admit that. Capitol Hill was for yuppies and hipsters.

"Do you feel comfortable there?" Ty asked

"Yes," Christine said slowly. She loved her underground apartment, even if it was little better than student housing. When she'd started methodically trying new things, one of the things she'd considered was moving.

But that had felt like too big a change. She'd have to find another underground place that was close enough to the bus line to get her into work. And cheap enough, too, which was getting harder and harder to find on the hill.

"I wonder…" Ty said, pausing. "Your power might be tied up someplace in the neighborhood."

"But where?" Christine asked. The neighborhood was awfully big. "Would some kind of finding spell help?" Though Christine couldn't cast the spell herself, maybe Tina could.

Ty shook his head. "Nope. Your power is hidden.

You'd be better off walking through the neighborhood every night, stumbling on it by accident."

"What would I do if I recognized one of these artifacts?" Christine asked.

Ty gave an expressive shrug. "Can't help you there, I'm afraid. But I will help you look. Different type of hunting. See if I can catch a trace of you where it doesn't belong."

"Thank you," Christine said politely. She wasn't hopeful. But she wasn't sure what else she could do but start the search.

Christine found that it was actually kind of nice to take a walk in the late evening, just as the sun was going down. She normally spent her time in her apartment, reading. Since the change, however, she had been finding herself growing more restless.

A nice, evening stroll seemed like just the thing.

Christine walked up Fourteenth Avenue, heading toward the bars and restaurants that lined Madison Street. There was a little café, actually, that she wanted to try. She'd put a book in her purse so she could sit a while and read. Dressed in comfortable, light-cotton black pants and a girl's T-shirt, scoop-necked with cap sleeves in lime green, she felt stylish. It fit her very well, as it should, as it was mostly illusion, like her human body.

The smell of freshly sawed wood filled the air as she passed one of the many sites where an old house had been torn down and developers were putting up four or eight (or more) townhouses instead. At least she thought they would be townhouses, and not more of those awful pod-apartments.

It was sad to see so many old houses torn down and replaced with ugly, cramped townhouses and apartments. However, many of the houses that were being torn down had needed more attention for years, decades, even.

Christine was glad, once again, that she didn't drive or have a car. Parking in her neighborhood had always been painful—she'd had to listen to Dennis complain about it often enough. Most of the new developments didn't have parking, so it would only get tougher.

What would happen if her powers had been bound to one of those old houses? Would they have been destroyed? She didn't think that would be how it worked, but she'd have to ask Nik or Ty or Tina about it.

What she wouldn't give for a complete library about how magical powers *actually* worked, instead of all the fantasy she'd read for decades.

The coffee shop was quiet, the lights dimmed for evening guests. They served beer, wine, and coffee after 5:00, making it a nice place to gather with friends. At least half the tables were empty: Christine guessed the café would be packed once school started again in a week or so.

After getting her iced coffee, Christine wound her way through the wooden tables and chairs, all the way to the back where two large wing-back chairs stood. A small, solid wooden table squatted between them. Both the chairs were empty, and the table had been cleared.

Christine settled in, pushing herself into the brown vinyl cushions. The chair had been made to look like leather, but this place couldn't afford that. Plus, it didn't smell like leather, just plastic. At least they wiped it down often enough that Christine could only catch a passing scent of the previous guest.

The grinder for the beans hummed. The soft hissing of steam followed. Christine normally liked places quieter than this, but it was peaceful here.

When Christine had thought she was human, she never would have gone out in public to read. She was too exposed, it wasn't safe, she'd get too lost in her book. Someone could have come up and stolen her bag and she wouldn't have even looked up.

Now, she could sit and read anywhere in comfort, knowing her troll senses would send up warning flags if someone got too close.

With a happy sigh, Christine sipped her drink and lost herself in windy hills that echoed with harp music.

Someone sat in the chair next to Christine. She didn't bother looking up from her book: the other person wasn't a threat. Plus, she had just gotten to the good part, where the harpist was about to break out of the magical prison that had held him, bound his power.

She could do that. Escape from whatever was binding her.

"Christine?" came a soft voice.

Christine grew very stiff. She should have known if a friend had sat down next to her, or someone she knew.

Was she losing more of her powers? Could she not rely on her trollish senses?

Slowly, Christine put her finger in her book to hold her place (though she knew where she was—this wasn't the first time she'd read this book) and put her other hand on the cover, as if to protect the book before she looked over.

She couldn't help her gasp.

Lars Sorgenfrey sat beside her. He looked pale—more pale than his usual pasty white, with blond hair and blue eyes. Many girls thought he was cute, though Christine had always just found him cruel, and thought that was reflected in his looks, with his beady eyes and thin lips. At least he'd stopped trying to grow a beard. It had never been more than a few patchy hairs. He wore his usual clothes. A T-shirt that said, "Marie Antoinette called. She says we're out of cake." Jeans. Brown leather loafers without socks.

"What are you doing here?" Christine asked, her voice gaining in volume. Lars had been one of the demons behind kidnapping Tina. He'd been sent to prison. She'd thought his sentence had run for years, not for a mere six months.

"Don't worry," Lars said, sitting back. "I'm not really here, you know."

Christine didn't know. She looked closely at him. While he appeared to be sitting in the chair, there was no indentation in the vinyl, as if he had no weight. She sniffed at him. She couldn't catch his scent at all.

"Are you a ghost?" Christine asked. While part of her hoped he hadn't been killed in prison, the trollish side of her would have been okay with his death.

He grimaced at her. "No, you aren't that lucky," he

said sourly. "This is just a projection. I'm allowed visitation rights, you know."

Christine hadn't known. "Do I need to get a restraining order or something?" she asked. She couldn't help the growl in her voice. Didn't really care.

"I'm not here to harass you," Lars said. He held his hands open wide, as if to show he wasn't armed. "I'm here to help you."

"Yeah, right," Christine said. "And why would you do that?"

"Because I've seen the error of my ways," Lars said piously. He brought his hands together into a prayer position over his chest.

Christine sighed. Lars had always been a smartass. Luckily, she didn't have to put up with him anymore. She stood up, determined to leave.

"No, wait," Lars said. "Don't go." He didn't sound contrite. That would have been faking it. Instead, he sounded tired and angry.

Christine looked back at him. He did appear to be tired. Dark circles bruised his skin under his eyes. Lines she hadn't noticed before marked his face. "Jail not suiting you?"

Lars paled more. He swallowed, hard. For a moment, his eyes looked haunted.

It appeared he *was* suffering.

Good.

Then Lars shook it off, his usual smirk resurfacing. "I can't just project somewhere else. I can only be here, and only for a short while. And it cost a lot of money to track you down. See what you'd been up to."

"So why should I listen to you?" Christine asked. She was certain that having her followed was against the rules of his confinement.

The good news was that if he'd paid to have her followed, that meant the protection charms in her apartment were working and he couldn't just appear there.

"Because I know where your powers are bound," Lars said.

Powers? Did she have more than one? And how did he know about her troubles with magic? Had he seen her at Nikolai's shop? And did he actually know something about her powers? Christine wasn't sure.

But she wouldn't find out anything until after he'd said his piece.

"Okay," Christine said, sitting back down in the chair. "I'm listening. But only for a short while. Talk."

Lars raised one eyebrow at her in surprise. "You've certainly taken to being a troll, haven't you?"

Christine merely growled at him, impatient.

"Troll magic is elemental, right?" Lars said. "Earth, of course, but also fire, air, and water elements."

Christine nodded impatiently, as if she already knew that, hiding the thrill she felt at learning that she had not one, but four powers, each tied to an element.

"Each of your elementals is bound in a different place. You're going to find them around the city by compass points—north, south, east, and west," Lars continued.

That actually made sense to Christine. It was one of the things she'd noticed since the changeling spell had broken. She could always figure out where she was, at least in regard to the cardinal points. She could spin around with her eyes closed, point in the direction she thought was north. When she opened her eyes, she'd invariably be right.

She figured that was because as a troll, she'd spend most of her time underground. She would have to know which direction she was facing without external clues like the sun rising.

"So where are they?" Christine asked. "And why are you helping me?"

Lars shot her a calculating look. "My family, well, I wouldn't go so far as to say we're in disgrace. That would be melodramatic. My mother might say that, but that's her."

Christine nodded. She'd never liked Mrs. Sorgenfrey either. She'd always looked down her nose at Dennis and Christine and the rest of the Tuckermans. Mum was friends with her, but then again, Mum tried to be friends with everyone.

"However, we aren't as high-ranking as we once were," he admitted.

"Good," Christine said. "That's what happens when you kidnap people and try to pervert their Destiny."

"No, that's what happens when you fail," Lars told her seriously.

"How will helping me get my powers back raise your family back up?" Christine asked. She wasn't sure she wanted her magic back if it meant that it helped Lars.

"It won't," Lars said.

Christine was about to tell him he was a liar when he held up his hand and continued. "What it *will* do is hurt the demon who bound you. His family and mine have had this feud going for generations."

Why had demons been involved in binding her powers? Christine really didn't like the sound of that. What kind of conspiracy had she uncovered?

And was Lars telling the truth?

"I'm not sure I believe you," Christine said slowly. "Who is this demon?"

Lars gave her a dry laugh. "Even if I told you his name, it wouldn't mean anything to you. Tell your friend the demon hunter that you're going after Ming the Merciless." He laughed again at whatever in-joke he was making.

"Not funny," Christine told him, fuming. "You have three seconds to tell me where my powers are bound. Or else I'm leaving and reporting you to the court." She was certain he was breaking some kind of law by contacting her.

Or maybe she would have to get a restraining order against him. The court could protect her against astral projections, couldn't it?

Lars seemed to realize that Christine was serious. "You need to start in the south, first. At the old fire station. On Eighteenth and Columbia."

At Christine's blank look, Lars gave an exasperated sigh. "You need to get out more."

"And?" Christine said when he didn't continue. "Where are the rest?"

Lars gave her a sly grin. "Patience," he said. "Get the first of your powers back. Then we'll talk."

He faded then, like the light on a film projector slowly

dying. In moments, he was gone. A subtle hint of ozone tainted the air around where he'd been sitting.

Damn it. Was he telling the truth? Who would she hurt by getting her powers back? Was it worth being magical if it helped Lars and his family?

She had the feeling that Lars wasn't telling her the whole truth. There might be some kind of feud going on between his family and this demon's, but there was something else, too. Were her powers some kind of political football, being passed between much bigger players?

She wasn't certain she cared. It was her ball.

And she wanted it back.

CHAPTER 3

Christine paced in her living room, automatically winding her way through the piles of books. The brown carpet was warm under her bare feet. She had to be careful when she walked on it with her troll feet, or she'd accidentally rip the carpet with her claws.

Bookcases lined the walls, also overly full with books. She'd refinished her bookcases after they'd been vandalized by demons. She hadn't been able to sand away all the gouges they'd scratched in the wood, but that was okay. They just reminded her that there was more to her life than what appeared on the surface.

Long, skinny windows ran around the tops of the walls, near the ceiling. Her apartment was considered "garden level" as it was mostly below ground. Christine had always preferred being below the earth. After the changeling spell broke, she'd understood why: trolls spent their lives in tunnels.

Outside, the soft swish of cars had died down. No one walked by on the sidewalk. It was quiet. Peaceful.

It was late, close to midnight. But Christine didn't feel tired. She kept pacing and pacing. She would probably regret not going to bed come morning. She'd be dragging all day at work.

She couldn't let go of the thought that she needed to go see if Lars was lying. She wanted to walk up to that fire station right then. The internet had told her that it had been Fire Station Number 23 at one point, but she hadn't been able to find much more information on it. She'd have to go digging through the archives when she got to work.

What would she find? Would she be able to free the element that was there? She assumed that it would be related to fire, since it was a fire station.

She wasn't afraid of walking around in the neighborhood on her own so late at night. If anyone tried to bother her, well, they'd get what they had coming to them. She might appear human, but she'd continued to train at the gym with Patrick the ogre. She was learning how to fight, and she was a lot tougher (and stronger) than she looked.

But what if this was a trap?

Christine wouldn't put it past Lars to try to trick her, to hurt her. She had put his ass in jail, foiled his plans to twist Tina's Destiny and start the endless Great War.

Christine didn't want to bring someone with her in case it was a trap. But she also didn't want to just disappear, or die mysteriously. To have some random jogger find her body on the sidewalk. Someone would need to avenge her, and she wanted to make sure that the blame was solidly placed on Lars.

In the end, she left an email for Dennis, telling him

where she was going and who he should blame if she didn't survive. He'd read it in the morning. That way, someone would know where she was going.

If she was successful, she'd send Dennis a second email later, telling him to ignore the first.

If she wasn't, well, Dennis would do everything he could to make sure that Lars suffered more.

It was the best she could do.

The night had finally grown cool. Christine could smell the water on the air, a marine layer sneaking into the city. She knew better than to hope for rain. They were in the middle of a drought that had gone on for far too long.

Traffic was sparse on the main roads. If it had been a weekend night, there would have been more cars. All the houses she passed as she walked up the hill were dark. Since school hadn't started yet, there weren't even students pulling all-nighters.

Christine turned down Eighteenth Street. She walked by a huge old church that was in good condition, made of dark red brick with white stone curlicues around the windows and cornices under the roof. Next to it was a girls' school, built later, she'd guess, but made to look like the old church.

There was money there, to maintain those kinds of buildings. Across the street, at least half of the houses appeared to be in as good a condition. However, there were also two of the old Craftsman houses that would probably be torn down as the neighborhood continued to gentrify. Three of the houses had already been replaced by modern, ugly townhouses. At least they'd kept most of the trees and greenery.

The old fire station stood on the next block. Christine's heart started pounding. She knew Lars hadn't been lying about the building. She'd seen pictures of it on the internet.

However, that was different than actually seeing it with her own eyes.

It was no longer a working fire station, but had been turned into a community center and food bank. Red bricks made up the walls, placed the long way, interspersed with smaller black bricks. It looked solid to Christine. Immovable. Like it had always been there.

Just past the fire station stood a park, with swings and a jungle gym. Plus what looked like a long fire truck made out of curved metal, for kids to climb on. Beyond the play area was a wide green meadow, shaded by old trees. At the far end were a couple of picnic benches, the perfect place to spend a lazy summer afternoon.

Christine slowly walked all the way around the park, then around the building. The fancy brick was only along the first third of the side of the building facing the park, then it changed to regular brick. Tall arched windows, all dark, looked at her with blank eyes from the side. The back of the building was even less fancy, the windows mere squares.

Returning to the front of the building, Christine drew back, standing on the curb, trying to take in the whole thing. It was two stories high. The doors had been squared off, but at one point, had been arched, probably for horse-drawn fire trucks. The building felt that old.

Christine didn't feel drawn to the building. She didn't feel repulsed by it either. She thought it was kind of cool looking. She was looking forward to learning more about it, searching through the archives at work.

However, she didn't have a clue where she might find her elemental power. Was it tied up inside? She didn't want to have to break in. It wouldn't be buried in the park either.

On the far right of the building, two large, arched windows had been bricked over with modern, plain brick. Christine let her eyes wander over the entire front of the building again. She kept being drawn by those windows. Was there something there? Then her eyes would skip away again, her attention drawn by the archways or the sign over the door or even the tall roof.

The longer Christine stood there, the more ridiculous she felt. What was she supposed to do? Call out, "Here, powers, come here!" like she would call a dog?

Lars hadn't been lying about there being an old fire station. But was he lying about there being something magical about it? Why hadn't he at least given her a clue about how to free the element bound up there?

It had to be her fire element, bound at a fire station. Should she light a match?

With a sigh, Christine approached the building. She was going to try using her magic and drawing... something, using her hands, like she had with the pile of dirt. She glanced up and down the street. She didn't see anyone, didn't hear anyone. She shook off her human illusion, going back to her natural troll state.

The night brightened, suddenly, as if a light had been turned on. She hadn't realized that her illusion of her human form had affected her senses so much. The air held more scents as well, the wet grass, the wood chips covering the playground, the leftover smoke from the grills at the far end of the park.

Christine walked closer to the two bricked-over windows. They were identical as far as she could tell. But she felt…less about the one at the corner of the building. The other one sparked her curiosity.

Was the far window enspelled to make sure she felt neutral about it? She contemplated the two windows. Yes, she definitely felt differently about them.

Eagerly, Christine stepped back and raised her hands. They weren't as cupped this time, her fingers more widespread. Slowly she rotated her hands until her wrists were facing each other.

She took a deep breath.

Here went nothing.

"What are you doing?" came a voice from behind her.

Christine turned, startled. Damn it! Why hadn't she sensed someone coming up? Were her troll senses messed up?

Then she saw who it was.

Dennis, her brother, had come.

"What are you doing here?" Christine asked as Dennis hurried up. So much for her plan about him not reading his email until morning.

"Good to see you too," Dennis said. He looked her up and down. "Is this really, uhm, necessary?" he asked, waving a hand at her.

Christine looked down. She wore a plain black T-shirt and shorts. What was he complaining about? Then she realized that he meant her trollish self.

Her feet were huge, much larger than his, even, with long sharp claws instead of regular nails. Muscled calves went up from there, covered in dark green skin that was completely smooth. More like a leathered hide. Her thighs were just as muscular, strong enough that she could run incredibly fast, but only for short distances. She was built for endurance—strength, not speed.

The rest of her was equally muscular and green. Large tusks grew up from her bottom jaw, over her top lip. Smaller fangs grew down, and her teeth were ragged. Not neat, precise, or pointed like fangs. They were meaner. Tougher. She'd leave any enemy with wicked bite marks.

Her new mouth had taken some getting used to, but now she could eat and not end up spilling food down her shirt.

Christine looked back up at Dennis. "It is," she said simply. "I need to be in my troll form." She couldn't do this without being her true self. Her brother didn't seem to get that. When the changeling spell had first broken, he'd been intent on "fixing" her. Though he'd finally come to accept that this was who she was, it still made him uncomfortable sometimes.

That didn't mean he wasn't her family, and wouldn't support her.

"So again, what are you doing here?" Christine asked. For the first time that night, she was nervous. She suddenly felt as though she didn't have much time.

"You said you were coming here to free your powers," Dennis explained. "I'm here to help."

Christine couldn't help her snort. "How?" It wasn't as if he knew anything more than she did about magic. Plus, he was merely human. Delicate.

What if something went wrong? She'd never forgive herself if he ended up getting hurt.

"Please," Dennis said.

Why did he feel he was entitled to roll his eyes at her?

"You can't see past the end of your nose, sometimes," Dennis pointed out. "I'm here to be a second set of eyes for you, to show you the obvious."

"Oh," Christine said. That might actually be helpful. She did ignore what was right in front of her occasionally, particularly when she was focused on something else.

"Plus, you shouldn't have to do this alone," Dennis added. "I'm your family. I'm here to help."

"And if something goes wrong?" Christine asked. Mum would never forgive her either if she got her brother killed.

"You're better than that," Dennis said. "Or you'll make it right."

Why did he have such faith in her? It didn't make

sense to Christine, though she was warmed by the sentiment.

"You stay behind me," she growled. "And if anything starts coming after you—run. Promise me that." Her family had always kept their promises. It was something Mum and Dad had taught them when they were kids.

Saying "I promise" meant something if you were a Tuckerman.

"I promise," Dennis said.

Christine quickly checked his hands, to see if he'd crossed his fingers or something to take away the truthfulness of his spoken words, as he often had when they'd been kids.

"Sheesh," Dennis said, holding up his hands, his fingers spread wide when he realized what she was doing. "If something is coming after me, that means it's gotten through you. You better believe I'm running."

"Good," Christine said. She shrugged her shoulders, feeling as if she was about to step into the ring with a demon. Her heart pounded in her chest. Her ears throbbed. She shook her head. Had her tusks just grown longer? Her claws sharper? What kind of a battle was she facing that she felt as though she had to armor herself?

Christine turned to face the building. She planted her feet wide, feeling the earth beneath her, solid and steady. She held out her hands.

"Here goes nothing."

Christine focused all her attention on the bricked-over window in the corner of the old fire station. Was that some kind of attraction that she was feeling? Before, she'd felt completely neutral about the window.

Christine felt the energy building inside her. She wasn't sure how she was doing it, but it was like she was drawing…something…from the earth beneath her. She widened her stance. The claws on her feet dug into the blacktop. The smell of rain filled the air.

When she'd first walked into the back room at the store, she'd been instantly attracted to the pile of dirt Nikolai had put there.

She now felt something similar. An attraction. A rightness.

However, it wasn't the bricks that were calling her.

It was something behind them. Something long buried and just now waking.

Dennis gasped.

A swirling pattern appeared in the center of the bricks, blue and glowing brightly in the night. The symbol was familiar to Christine. Where had she seen it before? It looked like a treble clef with added swirls and loops though the middle. Almost a compass rose, but skewed.

The bottom loop of the symbol glowed more brightly than the rest of it. Christine focused her energy there.

Lars had said the fire station held the southern element of her powers.

Christine found herself doing a strange balancing act between pushing and pulling, pushing herself, her trollness, her very *being* toward the wall. She felt her tusks and tough hide, her long claws, all the physical bits of her. Plus the elements of her personality that were pure troll, her growls, her affinity for the earth, her independence and stubbornness.

At the same time, she had a very tenuous hold on a thin, slippery piece of magic connected to the wall. It felt like pulling a wet hair out of a tangled knot, knowing that if she pulled too hard, she'd break it. She couldn't just grab hold and yank. She could only tug, gently.

She found herself growling at how long it was taking, at how the thread was thinning. It was going to break soon. She didn't know how to make it go faster, or to draw more out. Or how to make the thread thicker, either.

Did she have to light a match or something? Maybe Dennis had a lighter on him…

The thread grew even thinner. Christine stopped pulling so hard, growling louder.

Then she noticed the smell of rain had increased. It reminded her of fresh, spring rain, that brought the good smells of the earth with it.

Christine suddenly realized her mistake.

A demon wouldn't bind a fire elemental to a fire station. It was likely to grow and get out of hand.

It might, however, bind a water elemental there.

Christine found herself thinking longingly of the Seattle rain. It had been so hot that summer. She yearned for the mists that came and went, blessing her skin with water, then fading, then coming back. The way the rain sounded when big fat drops plopped on the ground just outside her windows. How it smelled cold in the winter and fresh in the summer. The concrete under her feet growing cool and moist in a sudden downpour. How the cars sloshed through the puddles. The sound of the water rushing down the gutters.

The thread Christine pulled on grew thicker, like rope. Then suddenly, instead of a single rope drawn out of the center of the skewed treble clef symbol, it became a handful of ropes that sprang from each looping end of the symbol.

The symbol itself glowed even brighter.

Christine grabbed hold and tugged, wrapping the threads around her fists. They grew more solid and she *pulled.*

The weight Christine pulled against suddenly evaporated and she landed hard on her butt.

Water came gushing out of the wall. A great deluge. The blast pushed her back further, so she was flat on her back.

The water kept coming. It drenched her skin, but most of it didn't slide off. Instead, it soaked directly into her. Her skin took the water like long dried earth, drinking it up. She found herself opening her mouth and gulping down as much of the water as she could, as if she'd spent months in a desert and this was the first oasis she'd found. It tasted sweeter than regular water, cool and divine.

Just as quickly as it had started, the onslaught dried up. Water stopped pouring from the building. Not even drops remained.

Christine pushed herself up to sitting.

Dennis was immediately at her side. "Are you okay?" He reached out a hand tentatively to touch her arm. "You're dry," he said with wonder.

Christine shook her head. A few drops still clung to her short hair, but that was it. Even her clothes were dry.

The night seemed lighter. Hell, *she* seemed lighter. More buoyant.

Yet at the same time, deeper. The earth beneath her held a song that she could just barely hear, now. The stars, too, sang lullabies. The night was more alive than it had ever been before.

Christine leapt to her feet. She wanted to dance, to sing, to throw her arms over her head and howl for joy.

But they were in the middle of a neighborhood. There were far too many humans around.

Instead, Christine took a deep, satisfied breath of air, filling her lungs, then letting it out slowly.

"Oh, Dennis," Christine breathed. "I'm so much better than okay."

~

Christine looked at the fire station with dismay.

The bricked over window that had held her power was now covered in graffiti. It looked as though someone had gone crazy with a spray can of white paint.

Underneath lay her looping design, buried below the rest.

Then there were harsh letters. Angular and caustic. Symbols that had no meaning to her but she knew weren't good. Nothing in English, or any language she at least recognized now—including several of the non-human tongues.

"Take a picture," she told Dennis as she dug out her own phone.

Dennis obediently took several shots.

Christine did as well.

Were those symbols part of the incantation that had bound her power in the first place? She didn't know.

But if they were, well, she could now believe that it had been some kind of demon spell.

Maybe Lars hadn't been lying. At least not about that.

~

"What?" Christine growled at Dennis.

He continued to stare at her.

They sat in his car in front of her apartment. Christine would have been perfectly happy walking home alone, but Dennis had insisted on driving her the few blocks. He seemed concerned.

The night still called to Christine. She longed to be out in it. Not in the city, no. But someplace wooded and primal. Someplace where it would just be her and the stars and the trees and the grass. Someplace where she could set a huge bonfire and dance around it.

Possibly naked.

Christine honestly didn't know who would be more shocked if she told Dennis that part—him or her.

"You're…different," Dennis said slowly.

Christine wore her illusion charm, so she at least appeared human, she knew. Olive-toned skin, a human face with regular teeth and eyes, short hair, plain T-shirt and jeans.

"What?" Christine asked with some alarm. "Is my appearance slipping?" That wouldn't do at all. She needed to look human, to fit in. Mostly.

It wouldn't do to *troll out* in front of anyone.

"No, no, you look the same, physically," Dennis assured her. "But…"

"Yes?" Christine asked impatiently when he didn't continue.

"There's something different," Dennis said finally. "I think it's your eyes."

Christine flipped down the visor on her side of the car, looking in the mirror on the back of it. She didn't see anything different about her.

"They aren't glowing," Dennis said after another moment. "But they are. There's more life in them."

Christine flipped the visor back up, sitting back in her seat, nodding. "That makes sense. I'm more, well, *me*, now."

"How does it feel? What just happened, exactly? Does this mean you can do more magic now? What kind of magic?" Dennis asked excitedly.

"It feels, it feels good," Christine told him. It was hard to explain. She would think that after just taking that much water into her system that she'd slosh or something. But that wasn't how it felt at all.

"I feel lighter," she told him. "Yet more connected to the earth. I'm more whole."

Now that she had her water elemental back, she felt the holes where the other elements went, where she was no longer as complete. Not as precise as a child's puzzle with the pieces missing, it was fuzzier than that. But she could recognize that there were empty spots inside her.

"As for the magic," Christine told him. "I have no idea." Tina had to be taught magic. Nikolai had assumed that Christine had to be taught as well. That she would have to learn spells and charms and incantations.

Christine assumed that was true for some of the greater spells. Or for turning mundane items magical.

But she was also a magical being. There should be some magic she could just do innately. Or maybe she had to be taught all of it, since she hadn't grown up with her powers.

She gave Dennis a grin, then held out her hand, palm up.

Could she raise a light now?

Christine focused all her energy and power on her hand.

A flame leaped up with a *whoosh*.

Christine jumped, startled, then dampened it down, but not before it scorched the ceiling of Dennis' car.

"Sorry," she said, though she didn't extinguish the light.

The flame in her palm glowed with the same blue as the sigil on the wall.

What else could she do now?

"Jeez," Dennis said. "Be careful with that thing!" He glanced over his shoulder warily as a car drove past them. "I should make you clean that up," he added as he peered at the scorch mark on the interior of his car.

"Sorry," Christine said again as she put out the light.

"It's just—it just feels so good, you know? To finally be able to do things." To cast magic like the characters she'd read about her entire life. To feel comfortable in her own skin.

"I've never seen you drunk before," Dennis said. "I'm worried about how you're going to handle it."

Christine bristled but didn't deny it. It was kind of like she was drunk.

"I won't let it go to my head," she said.

"Promise?" Dennis asked, serious.

Christine blinked. Was he that worried about her?

"I promise," she said solemnly.

Dennis visibly relaxed.

"Now, you need to get home. Get some sleep," Christine told him.

He gave her a grin. "Probably calling in sick tomorrow." He grew more somber. "You probably should too."

"But I feel great!" Christine said. "More than great," she admitted.

He nodded. "Yeah. I think you need to get used to this feeling first. Go slowly." He paused, then added, teasing, "And try not to burn down your apartment around your head."

Christine snorted. "As if. Not until I can make sure I don't hurt my books."

Dennis gave her a wide grin. "That's my sister. Books before people. I'll call you tomorrow, check in with you, see how you're doing. So pick up the damned phone. Okay?"

"I will," Christine said sheepishly. She didn't like the

phone that much, and often ignored it. "Night," she added as she opened the door.

"Talk with you later," Dennis promised.

He waited until she got in the door of her apartment building before he drove off.

Christine paused for a moment. It was oh so tempting to go back out, into the night. She wasn't tired at all.

But Dennis was right. She needed to get a handle on her new powers so she didn't accidentally, well, not *troll out.*

But maybe…*magic out.*

CHAPTER 4

Christine called in sick to work the next day. She'd rarely ever taken any sick days, and had a lot banked up. The last time she'd called in sick had been six months before, when the changeling spell had first broken, and she didn't know how to appear human anymore.

She didn't feel bad, though. She felt awesome. It was like getting an A on her final exam and winning the lottery and kissing the really cute troll boy, all at the same time.

She wasn't drunk with power. She still didn't have a clue what she could do with it.

There had to be something, though, that she could figure out on her own.

After Christine had called in to work, she drew herself a bath. It was one of the things she loved about her apartment: the claw-footed, extra-long tub. She could easily stretch out all the way in it, the gentle curve of it fitting both her human and troll backs perfectly. She put plenty of Epsom salts into the water. That always seemed to soothe her troll skin.

Christine leaned back in the water, breathing deeply. Her skin still buzzed. She hadn't been sure what it would feel like sitting in water, with all that water inside her. She couldn't help but be disappointed that it felt the same. She wasn't suddenly drawn to water, didn't feel an affinity for it.

She still should be able to do *something* with it.

First, Christine pulled the light back up into the palm of her hand. It came easily. She doused it, then brought it back again, teaching herself just how much she had to focus on it, how much of her will it needed.

Not very much, it turned out. She could just think about the light appearing, and it did.

Huh. No wonder Nikolai had been so frustrated that she hadn't been able to call up a light. Especially if it was supposed to be this easy.

Christine made the light she held bigger. She tried to shape it into a ball, but the best she got was an oblong blob with a bright tip at the end.

She looked around her bathroom. Pretty green-and-gold tile made up the top halves of the walls. The bottom was made of wooden wainscoting that always seemed to make the bathroom feel warm and cozy. Beige tile with matching gold flecks covered the floor in a decorative diamond pattern.

What would happen if Christine threw the fire? She remembered Dennis' warning about not burning down her apartment building. There wasn't much that she could burn, here.

With a careful but forceful lift of her hand, Christine tried to toss the fire in her palm toward the end of the bathtub.

The fire went out the moment it left her skin.

That wasn't useful at all.

Christine tried it again, this time with a smaller, more concentrated flame, about the size of a golf ball, burning much more brightly.

Exact same results. It appeared the flame had to be touching her for it to keep burning.

Could she shoot it from her hands? Call up a bigger flame like she had in Dennis' car?

She was much more successful with that. However, she found she couldn't turn her hand, raise her palm, and shoot fire. It appeared that the light needed something to rest against. So she could cup her hand and call a really bright light, and possibly burn something up to two feet away.

However, the way she had to hold her hand didn't feel natural. This wasn't how she was supposed to use this flame. Maybe it was just for lighting, and wasn't supposed to be used to attack.

What else could she do?

Christine contemplated the water in front of her. Her experiments with the fire (which did burn under the water, which was kind of cool) had kept the water warm, so she hadn't had to run any more.

Was there anything magical that she could do with the water?

Christine drew up some of the water in her palm and tried to mold it into a ball.

Nothing. It just flowed out from between her fingers, dripped down her arm.

Could she push the water to one side or the other?

Christine focused her attention and *pushed*, using both her hands, trying to move the water away.

For a moment, that seemed to work. The top two inches of water sloshed, as if suddenly hit by a strong breeze. Then the water bounced back and grew still again.

Awesome.

But how could she use it?

Christine laid her head back and thought for a moment.

On the one hand, the magic she felt wasn't fully integrated. It wasn't a water element, it was like she had a water elemental inside of her, who cooperated with her, not something she commanded.

On the other hand, once she got the hang of working with the water elemental, it probably wouldn't feel so separate from her.

Could she use her water elemental to find water? She doubted it. She didn't have an affinity toward it. But she could encourage it to move, one way or the other.

A strange thought came to her, about changing the course of a stream. However, it wasn't just the water. She'd have to be able to move the earth as well.

Suddenly, her power made much more sense. She should be able to move earth as a troll. Once she got her earth power back, she'd be able to tunnel and throw rocks and do all kinds of neat things.

Water wasn't her primary element. She would rarely work with it alone.

But if she worked with water in conjunction with the earth…

Christine jumped up, suddenly standing in the middle of her bathtub. She *had* to find her other powers. Had to learn everything she could, figure out all she could do.

Yes, she might be helping Lars and his family by breaking her power free.

But if she truly had all her powers, that might not matter.

She might be strong enough to beat him and make her way out of whatever trap he was laying for her.

Christine reasoned that if her water elemental had been the southern-most element, and if she walked straight north, she might run into the structure holding her northern elemental.

She had no idea what sort of building would contain what she presumed would be a fire elemental, the opposite of water. However, it wouldn't hurt to take a long walk up Eighteenth to see if she could find it, or see some clue about it.

Christine walked up the hill from her apartment to Eighteenth. The houses were mostly quiet, as it was the middle of the day and everyone was at work. There were a few kids out, playing in yards. She met more than one person walking their dog: a fierce, black-and-white Pomeranian princess with a blue ribbon in her hair, a lazy, slow red setter ambling along, as well as a hyper collie who wanted to slobber all over her hand.

The men she passed smiled at her, saying hello, their eyes drifting from her chest to her face and back down. More than one woman as well. It was Capitol Hill, after all.

Christine was too amused to be offended. *Everyone* seemed to have a smile for her that day.

Maybe Dennis had been right. Maybe she did look different.

The day was going to be stupid hot again. Christine was glad she was in a plain, brown T-shirt, a light-cotton black skirt, and sandals.

Six months ago, she never would have gone out of the house without being fully covered. Even in the heat of the summer.

Now, she felt as though she could wear cuter clothes. Clothes that didn't hide her. It didn't matter so much if people noticed her. She assumed that had been part of the changeling spell—that she never wanted to be looked at by anyone, never wanted to be noticed.

These days, she found she didn't care. It was another change for the better.

Christine actually smiled back, and shyly said hello, more than once. It made her heart beat hard every time. But nothing happened, either good or bad.

She could get used to this.

The houses changed as Christine walked north along Eighteenth, particularly after she crossed Harrison. She could see the affluence growing. Instead of smaller bungalows, or Craftsmen set on tiny yards that had been sub-divided, or new apartments stuffed in between, the houses grew bigger. They were better maintained. The yards, too, had fruit trees and lots of grass. More roses as well.

On the corner of Aloha and Eighteenth stood a huge Catholic church, done in white stone. The bell tower rang out the quarter hours merrily. Older brick buildings took up the southern corner of the block.

Christine paused as she looked at the building. Was this where they'd put a fire elemental? That didn't feel right. Why a church? Unless it was to desecrate it.

That didn't feel right either. Her powers weren't necessarily opposed to the Host. Just because sometimes *kith and kin* went along with the demons instead of the angels didn't mean she, or her magic, was evil. They were free agents.

And determined to remain so, at least according to Patrick the ogre.

Despite wearing a skirt, Christine was still unpleasantly hot. At the bottom of the hill, down on Nineteenth and Aloha, stood a coffee shop. She decided to go get an iced drink, then head back to her place.

Maybe she could get Dennis to drive her through the neighborhoods. She would also do more research on the buildings in the area. Since her water element had been trapped in a historic location, she would bet the others were as well.

However, there were *so many* old buildings along Eighteenth, Nineteenth, and the other streets as well.

Capitol Hill just had too much history.

Christine walked along the eastern side of Nineteenth, in the shade. A little business district had sprung up, with shops below three stories of apartments.

She'd have to come back sometime. Get ice cream at the cute little store there.

Maybe she could suggest that to Joe as a date. Walk up here and get something cool before they walked back to her place and got all sweaty again.

Christine found herself blushing at the thought and walked more quickly down the rest of the block, though no one was actually paying any attention to her. Not even the constant stream of joggers, all listening to their music as they put in their miles.

The buildings on the next block had at one point been a school, but had been transformed into a community building and park. She had to step to the side as moms with huge strollers passed her. Kids shrieked with delight in the park below her.

Christine paused at the steps leading down to the park. At the bottom splashed a large fountain. Fifteen jets of water shot up one after another, each at least ten feet tall. Other jets squirted from the large rectangular stones surrounding the center. Five columns about twelve feet tall stood in a circle between the water jets. Shimmering figures perched at the top of the columns: A man in a wheelchair lifting up a basketball; another man holding a baby high above his head, an older person reading, a young woman dancing and a young boy playing with a shooting star.

Christine slowly walked down the stairs.

If they'd bound her water elemental in a fire station, would they bind her fire elemental in a fountain?

She got more excited when she realized that the fountain itself was set up as a compass. Each of the large granite blocks around the columns had one or two letters burned into the top of them—N, NE, E, and so on.

A concrete bench circled the fountain on the east and south sides. A mom sat there, rocking a stroller back and forth while watching her two other kids playing in the water.

Christine sat down a little ways from the woman. They smiled at each other. Hesitant, Christine reached down and slid off her sandals, putting them on the bench beside her.

The woman gave her an encouraging nod.

Feeling daring, Christine pushed her feet forward and wet her toes in the spray of the water.

God, that felt good.

And Dennis would probably not believe her when she told him about it, that she'd actually done something like take her shoes off to play in a fountain.

It wasn't like the old Christine at all.

She splashed the water, thinking.

While the water felt good, she felt very *meh* about the fountain itself. She should have been excited about it. Or even curious about its history.

She looked northward, at the community building. It had been a school, once, made of old brick. She felt herself wondering about the community classes they'd teach there. Did they have a gym as well?

Then she turned back to the fountain. She was more curious about the building.

She felt strictly neutral about the fountain itself.

This *must* be the place. This must be where her fire elemental was bound.

Christine couldn't help herself. She surged up, laughing, her water elemental bubbling inside her. She kicked at the water with the side of her foot, a huge spray arching out.

It splashed one of the kids already playing in the fountain. Without hesitation, he splashed back.

Christine suddenly found herself in the middle of a water splashing war, giggling and getting wet. This was as close to dancing as she'd ever gotten, dodging spraying water and weaving in and out of the sudden jets.

Her family would never recognize her. She'd never done anything so spontaneous before.

But she was finally free of the changeling spell. Free to discover and be whoever she felt like being.

She couldn't wait to come back and free her fire elemental. To discover more of herself.

Christine spent the afternoon doing as much research as she could about the fountain. At one point, it had been a public wading pool. So it had been a water element for decades. She sat on her couch with her feet up, a glass of cool lemonade on the table beside her, her laptop in her lap. All the keys now had nicks from where she'd clicked them with her claws. The cover she'd gotten for the keyboard hadn't lasted for more than two days before she'd shredded it.

She couldn't afford a new laptop, so she tried to be extra careful every time she used it.

Maybe once she had her powers, though, she could

cast a protection spell on her keyboard. Which would be useful for a lot of things in her apartment, actually.

She'd have to remember to ask Nikolai about that.

Christine had to wait until later that night before she went back to the park, when there wouldn't be any people around. Again, she'd have to be in her native form to draw out the fire element.

Would the fire element be bound under the concrete of the fountain? She assumed it must be. She wasn't sure how she'd get at it, but since she'd been able to free her water element, she was confident it wouldn't take too much to release the fire element.

And if she could find all the others without any help from Lars…that would be kind of awesome. It would sure wipe that smug grin off his face the next time he came calling. And then maybe she could get a restraining order against him.

When Christine's phone rang, she sighed. Dennis had said he'd call. And she'd promised she'd answer.

She put her laptop down on the floor next to the couch and reached for her phone.

It wasn't Dennis.

It was Joe, her on again, off again boyfriend.

"Hello?" Christine asked. What did he want? What did she want?

"Hiya," Joe said cheerily. "How you doing?"

"Good," Christine said. It was true. She was doing good. Better than she ever had been.

"I'm surprised you answered," Joe said truthfully. "I'd figured you'd let it go to voicemail."

"I took the day off work," Christine said.

"What happened?" Joe asked.

Christine was touched by how worried he sounded. He knew that, as a troll, she didn't actually get sick.

"I, ah, found out that my magical powers are bound," she said after a moment.

"Okay," Joe said slowly. "What does that mean?"

Joe had always been uncomfortable with her being magical. She'd never been exactly certain why. He hadn't volunteered anything, and she'd always felt too shy to ask.

"It means that someone took them from me," Christine said. That still made her angry. "And I'm finding them and getting them back." She tried to keep down the growl.

"Cool," Joe said. "How can I help?"

Warmth flushed through Christine, making her feel happy. And wanted.

Joe might not understand her being magical, and it might make him uncomfortable, but like her family, he would support her.

Plus, as a troll, he was likely to be just as pissed off as she was that someone had stolen her powers and bound them. Merely on the principle of the matter.

So Christine told him about the previous night, finding her water element, and where she thought her fire element was bound.

"I take it you're going after your fire element tonight?" Joe asked. He sounded disappointed.

Christine hesitated. He would want to help, like Dennis. Did she want him there? "Yes," she said slowly.

"That's too bad. I won these tickets, at work, for

dinner and a comedy show. I was hoping you might be able to go."

"Tonight?" Christine asked.

"Yeah," Joe said. "It's a late show. Downtown. Doors don't open until 10:30."

"Oh," Christine said. The timing would work. She could probably go, if she wanted to. Then free her fire elemental afterward.

But she also knew herself. She wouldn't enjoy the show. She'd just be waiting for it to be over so she could go and do what she needed to.

That wasn't fair to Joe.

"I'm sorry," Christine said. "I can't." She paused, then added, "You understand." Her powers were more important.

Joe sighed. "There's always going to be something coming between us, isn't there?" He sounded angry.

"I don't know," Christine said. She honestly didn't. She didn't know how any of this worked, not dating, or being in a relationship, or being a troll in a human world, or finding and having powers—none of it.

"Okay," Joe said sharply. "I'll...I'll see you around." He hung up without another word.

Christine jabbed the phone off. Then cursed when she put (another!) scratch across the screen.

Damn it.

It wasn't her fault that all of this was so new to her.

Maybe after she got all her powers back she could call Joe. Ask him out for coffee or wine or something. Explain things to him, how different she felt. How right it was for her to have power. How good.

A little voice inside her head called her a liar.

~

Of course, the fountain was turned off at night. Christine cursed under her breath as she stalked around the tall columns. She'd assumed the water would be on and that she'd be able to draw her fire element out of it.

The night had cooled off, but it was still sticky and unpleasant. Christine had grown warm walking from her apartment to the park. She'd worn a black T-shirt and skirt, with her work boots, like some kind of goth. (She didn't consider herself cool enough to be a spy.)

Christine wasn't sure what she was going to do about her fire elemental. Did she have to figure out how to turn the fountain on? She really wasn't attracted to water, despite how she'd played in it that afternoon. She couldn't just call it out of the ground, even if she had reclaimed her water elemental.

Each of the large granite rocks that made up the compass points around the fountain also had jets in them that blasted water. Christine went back to the one on the northern side. A pillar stood directly between her and the center of the fountain.

Like the blocked-over window at the fire station, she felt strictly neutral about the granite.

Could her fire elemental be bound there, to the stone, instead of underground? No, that didn't make sense. Her powers had been taken and bound before the fountain had been built.

It was tied to the water, she knew.

Damn it! Christine stomped her foot in exasperation.

Crack!

Christine lifted her foot gingerly off the pavement. Had she done that? She hadn't meant to break anything…

"Hey!"

Christine slowly turned toward the west and the stairs. Of course Joe was ambling down them. He would be coming to help. She didn't know if she was happy to see him or not.

And that was a big part of the problem between them, wasn't it?

Joe sauntered down the stairs. Christine had to admit that he looked handsome as a troll, with broad shoulders and a cute nose above his tusks. His green skin was just a shade darker than hers, and the palms of his hands tended more toward brown than pink. He had similar claws for his nails, similar broken teeth, and ears that poked up higher than hers. (He couldn't move or swivel his ears either—a failing of her race, Christine still believed.)

"Hi, beautiful," Joe said as he came closer. He leaned in and kissed her on the cheek.

He smelled spicy, like cinnamon, and also like rich, fertile dirt.

Christine realized that was a huge part of her attraction to him—he always smelled comforting.

"Hi," she said. "You didn't have to come," she told him

honestly. She'd expected that she'd have to do this herself. It was part of why she hadn't exactly told the truth to Dennis when he'd called earlier that evening. She might have neglected to mention that she was going to try to free her fire elemental that night.

Joe shrugged. "I know." He shuffled his feet and looked distinctly uncomfortable. "Mom always used to say that magic was nothing but trouble." He took a deep breath. "And I'm the least magical of trolls. Got teased about it at school."

Christine felt her eyebrows rising to the top of her forehead. Joe rarely talked of his childhood, and even more rarely mentioned his parents. He'd left Trollville at a young age—and had joked about being kicked out of his house more than once. It was why he'd been in so much trouble when he'd first landed in Seattle with no money, no contacts, no friends. He'd ended up on the street for a while.

"I'm glad you're here," Christine said. She wasn't sure how he could help. It still meant something that he'd come.

"So what are you going to do?" Joe asked.

"I need to call the fire elemental up out of the water. It's underneath the fountain," Christine told him. She looked down, remembering the crack she'd heard.

Joe looked down as well. He gave a long, low whistle.

A crack in the formerly smooth concrete ran from where Christine was standing toward the center of the fountain, under the pillar. "Did you do that?" he asked. Then he gave her a toothy grin. "You're a lot stronger than you look, aren't you? Good thing I like 'em with muscles."

Christine snorted. Of course, Joe would be flirting with her. Then she turned serious, studying the ground.

She hadn't meant to crack the concrete. She didn't think that she normally would have the strength to do that.

However, maybe there was something magical involved here. Maybe it wasn't so much sheer strength as the fact that it was *her* here, doing it.

Christine walked slowly to the stone marked E, for the east, and stomped down with her foot again.

"Whoa, whoa!" Joe cried, rushing over to her. "What do you think you're doing?"

Another crack appeared, running directly from the stone to the center.

Christine sighed. She didn't want to destroy the fountain. It brought such joy to the kids in the neighborhood. She'd loved playing in it that afternoon.

Did she have a choice, though?

"It's the only way to get at my fire elemental," she explained to him.

"You sure?" Joe asked. "This is destruction of public property. You could get jail time. Or a fine. Or both."

Christine's gut knotted. She'd never even gotten a parking ticket. The time she'd been served papers for illegally traveling to a pocket world, in search of the demons who'd taken Tina, had been the first time she'd ever been in trouble with the law.

"I'm sure," Christine said after a moment. She still had that hole inside her. It bothered her, like a loose tooth, though it wasn't as well defined as that. Just an emptiness where her magic was supposed to go.

Christine walked over to the southern-most stone and stomped again, creating another crack.

"You ready?" she asked as she walked to the western stone. "You don't have to be here." He could leave and she wouldn't squeal on him. He didn't have to get in trouble.

"I was born ready," Joe assured her.

Christine still didn't know where that reference came from. She really was going to have to remember to look it up.

Crack!

The last split running across the concrete rang out louder than the first. It struck Christine in her bones, as if she stood inside a huge bronze bell that had just been rung.

Light poured out of the cracks—the same blue-white light that had come from the window at the fire station. The cracks widened and twisted, forming the same sigil. It still reminded Christine of a treble clef with extra swoops and swirls. She'd tried looking it up on the internet but hadn't found anything quite like it.

Where had she seen it before? Why was it so familiar?

A second, redder light sprang up beside the blue. Christine gulped when she realized that now a five-pointed star connected the five columns together, made from that red fire.

There had to be demonic energy at work here as well.

Christine hurried over to the northern-most point, holding out her hands, ready to form a cone of focused energy again.

But this was different than the first time. At the fire station, Christine had had to press as well as pull, to push her being into the wall, to get the water elemental to waken and recognize her.

The fire elemental burning in both the blue and red lighted cracks already knew it was her. Recognized her.

Didn't care.

All it wanted was to be free. It was fire.

If it went with her, it would be trapped again.

With a sinking heart, Christine realized that just freeing her fire elemental wouldn't be enough.

She was going to have to capture and tame it as well.

CHAPTER 5

"Look out!" Christine warned Joe as the fire surged out of the cracks in the concrete.

Joe leaped back just in time as a whip-like cord of fire snapped at him. Sparks hissed.

The quiet of the night was split by the roaring of the great fire. It grew taller than the fifteen foot columns, a great whirlwind of flame. It laughed at Christine as it gained power in the air, free from its fetters.

It was laughing at her, she knew. How could such a puny being as herself possibly hope to contain such a great being?

Christine still tried. She gathered a great ball of force and *pushed* out at the flames, trying to contain the fire elemental, to shape it.

The fire's cackling laugh spread all the way up to the stars. It loomed over Christine, threatening to scorch her to a crisp.

I'm free! it laughed.

All it wanted to do was burn.

Christine wouldn't have been as worried if it had been fall, and wet. But it had been an unreasonably warm summer with no rain.

If the fire elemental got off the concrete, it could set large parts of the city aflame, as all the grass was dry and straw-like, ready to flame at the slightest spark. So many of the trees, too, had brown leaves instead of their usual green.

She *had* to contain it. Now.

Christine pushed again, but she had no power to bind the fire elemental. No earth to contain it. Her water elemental wasn't enough to extinguish it.

The fire elemental lashed out at Christine, casting a stinging blow against her wrists, knocking her hands to the side.

Christine automatically turned and shoved back, blasting the fire elemental with power.

It wasn't enough to do any damage, but at least that got its attention. It stayed where it was, burning with fury, flames licking the sky, cackling with energy and fury.

Do your worst, it taunted.

Christine hesitated. This thing wanted a fight.

Could she destroy it? Maybe. Given enough time and power. However, that wasn't what she was supposed to do.

She needed to tame it.

"What are you waiting for?" Joe called. "Attack!"

Christine shook her head. No. That wasn't right.

Maybe some honey would work, calling like to like.

Christine raised her hands toward the whirlwind of flame, but instead of attacking with her palms out, she reversed her hands, moved her fingers down and cupped her palms, filling them with her own burning light. She extended it toward the fire elemental, like an offering.

Again, she felt like she was calling a dog. "Here, boy. Come here. Heel."

Or was that *heal?*

Tendrils of flame reached out from the whirlwind and wrapped around Christine's wrists.

Christine's skin *burned*. It didn't hurt. Not exactly. But it was suddenly hard to breathe in that heat. Sweat poured freely from her, down her face, her back, along her sides.

The fire elemental lapped up the flames Christine offered. She poured more power, more light, into her palms, feeding the elemental. The color of the elemental changed, growing cooler, more blue, less angry red.

Christine drew as much power as she could from deep inside of her, pushing it out toward the elemental. She found she was panting with the effort. It was like pushing a block uphill. Her muscles strained, her hands shook, but she was too stubborn to yield or take a break.

"What are you doing?" Joe asked. He sounded… concerned. But his voice came from very far away.

Christine stepped forward. The fire elemental sent out more tendrils, caressing her. Her blood grew warm, very warm, like she was stepping into a sauna and about to make love to the troll resting there.

Out of the corner of her eye, Christine saw Joe rush forward.

The fire tossed out a casual blow, throwing him back and away.

Christine had a moment of concern, then she was overwhelmed by the fire. It consumed her, caressed her, made all her skin come alive. All she smelled was the wonderful scent of burning pine, comforting and warm. Flames quenched her thirst for more—more touch, more sensation, more heat, more desire.

She walked forward to the middle of the fountain, standing in the center of the flames. She *burned*, alive, powerful, hungry. She spread her arms out wide, as if she was welcoming her lover home. The fire took over all her senses. She spoke flame as she tilted her head back and howled. Smoke hung from her arms like a grand cape. Sparks shot from her fingertips.

After a timeless time, Christine came back to herself, back to the earth and cold concrete, away from the land of fire. When Christine wrapped her arms around herself, they were empty. She only touched herself.

The flames were gone. They'd burrowed deep inside her.

They'd come home.

"Are you all right?" Christine asked as she walked over to where Joe still lay on the concrete.

"Yeah," he said slowly.

Christine grabbed his outstretched hand and pulled him easily to his feet.

Huh. Had the fire elemental made her stronger? Or was it because she felt more grounded now?

Joe's T-shirt had a ragged hole in the center of it, where the fire had burned him. Pinhole burns showed where sparks had landed on his jeans. His skin looked raw and red, though it wasn't blistering. (Did troll skin blister when it was burned?) He had a dazed look, as if someone had just smacked him hard.

Which, okay, maybe the fire had.

"What were you doing?" Christine asked as she led him to the chunk of granite that was the west side of the fountain, making him sit down so she could look at him. He still had a vacant look in his eyes.

"You were covered in flames," Joe said as he sat heavily. Wonder touched his voice. "I thought you were dying."

Christine bit her tongue. Maybe to an outsider it had appeared that way. But she hadn't been burning. Or at least, her clothes hadn't been on fire or anything.

He shouldn't have tried to interfere. He shouldn't be here at all. He needed to leave.

Christine recognized those feelings coming from the fire, still burning deep inside her. It resented Joe.

Pipe down, Christine tried to tell it.

The fire elemental grumbled but subsided.

"I was fine," Christine told Joe. "It was kind of awesome." She didn't know if she'd ever be able to express how completely the fire had touched her, how much it was, and always had been, a part of her.

It was like this whole portion of her had been walled away, iced over, and the fire had thawed it out.

It made her feel alive like she never had before.

It also made her more angry than ever that this had been taken from her. That she'd been a mere shell of her true self for her entire life.

"Now what?" Joe asked quietly. "What are you going to do?"

Christine smiled at him. She thought about touching his shoulder, but she held herself back. She still burned. And though he kind of smelled right, like good dirt, he also smelled wrong. Not like a human, but too much like *other*.

She didn't know where that scent came from, but it sent warning shivers down her spine.

"I think," Christine said after a pause, "that I need to spend a couple of days actually getting used to this power."

While a part of her *hungered* for her other powers, the earth and wind elementals, the gaps aching inside her, she also felt unbalanced. She was hot and cold. Too much and too little. The power sloshed around inside her. If she bent over too far, would she just fall over?

"You need some help?" Joe asked, giving her a broad wink. "Getting acquainted with that skin of yours?"

"No, thank you," Christine said, pulling away. "I need to do this on my own."

"What, you aren't even going to let me watch?" Joe teased as he stood up.

Christine snorted. "Not this time," she told him.

"Then maybe the next," Joe said. He looked over at the fountain. "Did you do all that?" he asked.

Christine turned back toward the fountain. Again, harsh graffiti now covered the place where her fire elemental had been. Her sigil was there, buried in the center of it. The red pentagram connecting the pillars was there as well. White, stark tags marred the compass stones. Ugly symbols sprawled over the concrete.

Deep cracks marred the ground too. They stank of

refuse, as though she'd broken a sewer line.

"I swear to you, those aren't mine," Christine told Joe fervently.

Neither of the elementals inside her recognized them.

"I think those are demon markings," Joe said slowly.

Christine nodded, fishing out her phone. She took pictures of them. She would go to the store the next night and show Nikolai.

Those markings weren't good. Were they inherently evil? She wasn't sure. They were, however, related to the magic that had bound her power.

Why were they there? What being had actually bound her elements?

And why had someone stolen her power to begin with?

Christine had more questions than answers.

However, at least she now felt as though she had more resources at her fingertips, more magic that she could use to go searching for clues.

Christine carefully knelt down next to the couch to pick up the book she wanted to read next, then gingerly placed herself on her couch again. Normally, she would have just reached over to grab it, however, she still felt top heavy. She was afraid that if she leaned too far in one direction or the other she'd topple over.

Work that day had been…interesting. Her co-workers had actually believed she'd been sick the previous day, not given how she looked (her illusion spell made her appearance perfectly normal) but how she moved, so cautiously, as if she were made of porcelain and would easily break.

Christine felt uncomfortable and overly full. Her fire elemental hadn't settled in like her water elemental. It sizzled under her skin, sending abrupt waves of heat coursing through her body. She'd broken out into a profound sweat while just sitting, more than once.

Was this what humans meant when they talked about hot flashes?

Plus, the smoke clouded her brain. It made it hard to think. And her sense of smell was now dull, tainted with smoke.

With her water elemental, Christine had been eager to practice, to try out magic, to see what she could do.

Now, she truly feared that she'd burn her apartment building down accidentally.

She put off seeing Nikolai that night. Maybe he could have helped, but she felt too off balance. She'd give herself another day of settling in before trying to work with this new power.

She also had the feeling that her fire elemental would continue to fight her when she tried to use it. Like a tricksy fairy godmother, it might give her exactly what she asked for magically, with horrible consequences that she hadn't considered.

Not even a long bath had helped.

Christine had just settled into her book, happily diving into the changing sea at the end of the world, when her phone rang.

Guiltily, Christine picked it up. She sighed with relief

when she saw it wasn't Dennis. She really should call him and tell him about getting her fire power.

It was Ty, the demon hunter.

Curious, Christine carefully swiped the phone on, luckily avoiding scratching the surface (again!)

"Hello?" she said.

"Hey, Christine." Ty's cheerful voice came over the line, making her smile. He'd remained a good friend, helping her negotiate between the human and other worlds.

If only he were a troll…

"You busy?" Ty asked.

Technically, she wasn't busy. She was just…recovering. "Not really," she said slowly. "Why?"

"Okay, then I'm coming to get you," Ty said abruptly. "You need to come see this. Be there in five."

The line went dead.

Christine brought the phone down slowly, looking at her hand. Should she call him back? Warn him away?

Ty had said he'd start hunting around the neighborhood, see if he could find a trace of her where she didn't belong.

Had he found another place where an elemental of hers was bound?

And did she want to get it, now?

∼

Ty was as good as his word and knocked on her door in about five minutes.

Christine was waiting for him. She didn't bother with

the three locks and the chain on her door anymore. Demons could just enter her apartment from a portal (though not in the living room where she'd hung the ugly protection charm she'd made). And anyone human breaking in deserved what greeting they got.

Not that she'd kill a human. Not if she could help it. But she was much more able to defend herself, now.

Christine was ready with her excuses. She was too tired. She felt overly full. She wasn't certain she should get another of her powers right now. She might not be able to integrate it well. She should wait until she'd gotten used to the others, first.

She also knew she was lying. She *hungered* for her missing powers. The hollow spots inside her ached for them. Now that she'd gotten back her fire and water elementals, she knew she'd never rest or be complete without the others as well.

Ty grinned at her from the hallway when she opened the door. He looked the same as always, with a sharp nose and kind eyes, his dark skin smooth under the lights. He wore a flat cap over his kinky black hair, a gray T-shirt that showed off his muscled chest, strong dark legs under his khaki shorts going down to Teva sandals.

Ty paused in the doorway, peering at her. He raised his nose and sniffed the air before fixing her with a sharp look. "You're different," he said. He stayed where he was, not entering her apartment.

"I found two of my magic elementals," Christine told him. "Water and—"

"Fire," Ty said, stepping across the threshold. "I can smell it."

"Can you?" Christine asked, curious. She gave a sniff herself. She'd been smelling smoke off and on since she'd gathered in her fire elemental. She'd also wondered if she'd been paranoid.

"Stay still, please," Ty asked as he walked all the way around her. By the time he'd reached her front again, his eyes were no longer human, but fully black and glowing with a blue tint. "You're a lot more powerful," he said.

Christine shrugged. She'd kind of figured that would be the case. It was part of why she didn't want to experiment with magic, at least not here, and not until she was more sure of herself.

Ty stood quiet, nodding to himself. He seemed to come to some kind of conclusion. "I think I know where another of your elements is bound."

"Really?" Christine asked. She couldn't help how eager she sounded, how excited that made her. Both the fire and water elements fizzed up inside her, like carbonated water and sparks thrown by a fire.

Ty nodded. "In the Arboretum."

"That's the huge park, east of here," Christine said.

At Ty's curious look, Christine added, "The water elemental was in the south. The fire elemental was to the north. Up and down Eighteenth, Nineteenth."

Ty nodded. "What I found is just inside the park. Near Madison. An old bridge that smells like you. A place of power."

Christine opened her mouth, then shut it again, shaking her head. She *wanted* to go see this bridge, to free her next power. It was like an itch that *had* to be scratched.

She wasn't certain it was safe, though. Or smart for her to acquire another power so soon, when she hadn't integrated the others. Not really.

"We'll just go take a look," Ty told her, forestalling her arguments. "You don't have to free the elemental tonight. I just want to show you where it is."

"I could do that," Christine said. It sounded like a good compromise to her.

She could just go and see the place where another elemental of hers might be bound.

She could resist freeing it immediately.

Right?

The park officially closed at sunset. It was just past that, the night growing darker, particularly when they crossed from the street to under the trees. Christine didn't have any trouble seeing in the dark, like most of the *kith and kin*. It didn't strike her as a wild place. It had been tamed by humans. A broad meadow spread out just past the trees, gradually sloping up to a hill covered in yet more trees. Christine imagined that during the fall it was probably gorgeous, with all the leaf colors.

She'd have to remember to come back later, though admiring the fall leaves did strike her as a particularly human thing to do.

Ty cut across the grass, not bothering with any of the paths. The grass was dry, stiff under Christine's feet.

They needed a good rain. And soon.

The smells of the night seemed muted. Was it because

all the plants had pulled back due to the lack of rainfall? Nothing was growing in this heat. Instead, all the leaves and twigs and grasses were wilting, browning, burning.

Or was it the smoke of her fire elemental interfering with her sense of smell?

Ty led her up a hill, into the trees, then out again, down a grassy slope.

He didn't have to point out the place to her. She could see it.

A small grassy area opened up after the hill. It sloped in the center to a dry bed of rocks. It was probably a significant creek during the wet season. Just past the riverbed stood what looked to be an ancient stone bridge.

The bridge had been built up on manmade earthworks. It wasn't very long, maybe ten feet. Or very wide—no more than three people could cross it, walking side by side. It rose up high in the air, twelve feet, at least. It arched sharply, as if ready for very tall beings to parade underneath it. It ran directly north-south.

It was very picturesque. Christine was certain that people would picnic on the banks of the creek when it was running, then take photos of themselves and the bridge. Possibly they would even get married there. It seemed like that kind of place.

While Christine had felt very neutral about the other locations, this place was different. She recognized it, despite never having been there before. She knew what the bridge would look like under moonlight. How cold the stones would feel in the rain. The sound of the creek running under it. How soft the moss was.

"What is this place?" Christine asked Ty, hushed. Also,

scared. How did she know these things? Was it the other elementals, the ones already inside her? Were they making her feel these things? Or was it something else?

He turned and looked at her, studying her. "It's a bridge," he said slowly. "And when I was here, earlier this evening, I caught a scent of you. Then it was gone. Too fast to trace. Then it came back, teasing." He shook his head. "It seemed strange. It wasn't right. There's something about this place that's different."

Christine nodded. A power of hers had been bound to this beautiful bridge. She just *knew* it. She didn't have to test her own feelings, or figure out how neutral she felt about the structure. It just felt…right.

Her power was buried deep in the stone of the bridge. She was impressed that Ty had caught even a trace of her.

Ty stepped beside her, then turned to face the bridge. "So is your earth elemental bound here?" he asked quietly.

"No," Christine said, almost immediately. The bridge was too connected to the earth. Though part of the bridge was in the air, the bridge itself didn't represent the opposite of the earth.

"Air," Christine breathed out after another moment. An air elemental would want to be free, able to go everywhere.

A bridge was always connected to the ground. Both ends, forever bound. Her air elemental could never escape, could never be free of the earth.

"How you going to free it?" Ty asked.

Not *are you going to*. But *how*.

Christine wanted to protest. Wanted to tell him that she wasn't going to do this now. That she didn't have any more room inside. She had to leave this one, at least for a little while. That she'd come back tomorrow, or the next day.

She knew she'd be lying, though.

There was something there. It didn't call her. It didn't recognize her. It was aloof.

It was still *hers*.

"I need to go up to the bridge," Christine told Ty. "I need to be standing in the center of it in order to free my power."

The night had grown sticky with anticipation. Cicadas sang, hidden in the grass, their cycling song urging Christine to move forward. Past the trees, the occasional swish of a passing car slid through. She still smelled nothing but smoke. Maybe the air elemental could blow that away.

Christine considered the bridge again. She'd end up destroying it, she knew, when she freed her power.

Hopefully, the fall wouldn't be too bad when the rocks let go.

Ty nodded. "All right," he said. He looked ready to go with her.

"No," Christine said. "You need to stay here. Out of the way. It will be dangerous."

The fire elemental had been bad enough, reaching out and smacking Joe, sending him flying.

This air elemental—Christine knew it wasn't just air, but wind. It would bring trees crashing down. They were in the middle of a wooded area. It could throw spears of branches at anyone threatening it.

"In fact—" Christine began.

"No," Ty said firmly. "I'm not leaving. I have a few tricks up my sleeve to protect myself. I'll be fine."

"Are you sure?" Christine asked, worried. She really didn't want Ty to get hurt.

"I'm sure," Ty replied. "Besides, it'll be such a great story if I get my ass handed to me by an air elemental."

"It won't be just air," Christine warned. "It'll be wind. And magic. And it's probably pissed off." The fire elemental certainly had been.

"You just worry about yourself," Ty said. "You need to survive this."

He sounded so sincere. Was it just because he was concerned about her? Or did he know something more about her and her powers? Something he wasn't telling her?

"I'll be fine," Ty said. "Now, go."

Christine nodded, hesitant. There was a small voice inside her head that said this was a bad idea. That she should wait.

But she'd waited all her life. Been waiting, really, just to die, before the changeling spell was broken.

It was time for her to live. For her to reclaim herself, her power.

It was going to be messy. Painful.

She still needed to do it.

Now.

CHAPTER 6

Christine headed for the left slope of the bridge. How old was this footbridge? It felt ancient to her. Like it had been here since the first settlers. Was the creek underneath at one point a raging river? She'd have to look up the history of the bridge later.

The night was still muggy, but Christine found chills going down her spine as she approached the bridge. She wasn't certain why. Were there already winds rushing to greet her? Colder air emanating from the stones? She still couldn't smell much beyond the smoke she carried with her.

When Christine was only a couple feet away from the left earthworks, a shadow detached itself from under the bridge.

Christine found herself automatically taking a fighting stance, one foot behind the other, her hands raised, her claws out, her weight sunk lower.

Joe resolved out of the darkness.

Joe?

"What are you doing here?" Christine asked. She lowered her hands but she didn't shift her feet. She was still ready to attack or to defend herself.

"You can't do this," Joe said, his voice low, the warning evident.

"What do you mean?" Christine said. "Can't do what? And did you already know that one of my powers was bound here?"

Ty was suddenly beside Christine. "You need help?" he asked.

Christine was happy for the backup, but she could take Joe.

Whether he realized that or not was an entirely separate question.

"I got this," she told Ty. "Go back down."

Ty had partially changed into his other form. His nose had pushed forward into a muzzle with sharp teeth. His hands, too, had grown claws. He didn't look as solid or as formidable as a troll, but as he'd said before, he had other tricks up his sleeve.

"You sure?" Ty asked, looking from her to Joe and back.

"I am," Christine told him.

"You call, I'm there," Ty told her. His ears had turned into something like a wolf's ears, perched high on his head.

Christine again felt a momentary pang of jealousy that he could swivel his ears. But it was good to know that she had backup.

"I will," Christine promised.

Joe and Christine waited until Ty had ambled away.

He stopped a little closer to the bridge than Christine felt comfortable with, but she didn't feel as though she could shoo him away, tell him to get to safety.

She wasn't sure what distance would be safe once she freed her air elemental.

Joe grabbed Christine's arm and started hauling her up the hill, toward the top of the bridge.

Christine suffered his grip until they got to the foot of the bridge. Then she stopped and stood completely still, refusing to go another step.

When Joe turned back, she looked pointedly at his hand still wrapped around her arm, then at him.

"Sorry," Joe murmured, though he didn't sound sorry at all. He glanced over his shoulder at Ty, as if making sure the demon hunter had stayed below. Then he glared at Christine. "Why did you bring *him* here?"

"I didn't," Christine said, bewildered. "He was the one who brought me here. Said he'd found a trace of my scent on the bridge."

"Oh," Joe said. His anger deflated a little. "So you didn't know about this place?"

"No!" Christine said, her own anger picking up. "What is this bridge? Why is it so familiar? It isn't just because my power is bound here, is it?"

Joe shook his head. "You really didn't know?" he asked, his full of curiosity.

When he didn't continue, Christine asked, exasperated, "Know what?"

"This is the fairy bridge. The start of the road to Trollville."

"Oh," Christine said. "How was I supposed to

know?" It wasn't as if someone had given her a pamphlet about all things trolls when the changeling spell had broken.

Joe shrugged. "I just figured you knew. Since you're magical and all."

Was that derision in his voice?

Christine felt her temper rising further. "Well, I didn't. Thanks so much for telling me." She moved to walk past him, onto the bridge.

Joe grabbed her bicep again to stop her.

Christine twisted her arm up while at the same time applying pressure to Joe's wrist, breaking his grip. She let go of Joe before she did something she might (or might not) regret later, like crushing the fine bones in his hand.

"What?" she asked angrily.

"You can't do this," Joe said again. "You can't free your power. You'll break the bridge. We'll lose the trail to the other worlds. Not just to Trollville. But to many of the *kith and kin* worlds."

"There's got to be more than one trail," Christine said reasonably. "Can't you just travel to Trollville? Through a portal? Like to a pocket world?" She'd always assumed that was how *kith and kin* traveled from their various worlds to the human world, through portals.

Joe stubbornly shook his head. "Portals aren't allowed. Too easy to ship an army through a portal, to invade. There are only the roads. Those are much easier to defend."

"There can't be just this road," Christine said. That would be stupid.

Joe sighed. "Yes, there are other roads. But none in this

region. You have to go to California, or New York, to find another one."

Christine would bet there were others beyond those, but she wasn't about to argue with him over that. "My power's bound here," she said instead. "My air elemental. It was *stolen* from me and bound here." She tried to keep her temper in check. Failed.

"I figured that was why you were here. To free another elemental of yours. But when you free an elemental, you destroy what it was bound to." Joe crossed his arms in front of his chest, taking a wider stance. "And I can't let you do that."

"You'd rather I stayed weak. Incomplete," Christine angrily accused him.

Joe shrugged. "I wouldn't, actually. I'd rather see you with all your powers. But you're one person. You're putting all of the *kith and kin* at risk."

Christine could see that. She honestly could.

But the ache inside her, the *need* for her magic, was stronger.

"Once I get all my magic elementals back, I'll be even stronger," Christine said slowly. "I'll be able to do a lot."

Joe nodded. He didn't seem impressed.

"How about this? I will repair the bridge once I get all my powers back," Christine told Joe. "I promise."

The words rang out, carried by winds Christine didn't feel. She felt as though a bell tolled deep inside the earth, marking her promise, making it as binding as the stone around her air elemental.

A promise had always meant something when Christine had been a changeling. It was a value her human parents had instilled. When a Tuckerman promised something, they meant it.

As a troll, the word she spoke had taken on much more meaning.

Joe blinked, startled. "Really?" he asked. His arms fell back to his sides. "You mean it. You'll fix the bridge."

Christine nodded. "After I get all my powers back," she told him. "I won't be able to do it until I have my earth power again." Just thinking about being able to sink her claws into rich, fertile dirt, to mold it to her will, gave her chills.

Joe nodded. "I still think this is a bad idea. And for anyone else, I wouldn't do this." He took a deep breath and stepped to the side. "But you'll keep your promise. You'll fix the road. Better than it was, yes?"

Christine nodded fervently. "I will. I promise."

Again, that ringing tone that she felt down in her very bones.

She didn't know what kind of work that would entail, but she knew it was important, not just to Joe, but to all the *kith and kin*.

"Then you shall pass," Joe said, his own words taking on a ringing quality. "And good luck."

"Thank you," Christine said.

She was surprised he didn't try to give her a kiss for luck.

Then again, she'd probably break his nose if he tried to touch her again.

Ever.

With a sigh, Christine marched forward. She didn't

feel ready to do this. She still felt overly full with her other powers. Out of balance.

Maybe even out of control.

She was still too determined, too stubborn, to walk away at this point. Even for a single night.

Well, here goes nothing.

That seemed to be her rallying cry.

W inds picked up and swirled around Christine when she reached the middle of the bridge. The stones felt wet and slimy under her feet, though there hadn't been any rain for weeks. A three-foot-high wall built of the same stone as the rest of the bridge ran along each side, keeping people from easily falling over.

Below her, to the west, a picturesque meadow opened up, edged by dark trees. She could see the remains of where the creek would generally flow, could easily imagine that it had once been a much larger, more angry river.

Christine reached out and touched the eastern wall of the bridge. The view there surprised her. She suddenly appeared to be up high in the mountains. Below her was sheer rock. Off in the distance, to the right, she could see an old-fashioned stone house, more like a cottage. It had a steep red-clay roof and tall, narrow windows. A thin trail of smoke rose up from its chimney.

The cottage appeared to be built out of the side of the mountain itself. It squatted directly on the stone path leading away from the bridge. No one could continue around it—on one side was the steep ridge, dropping off to nothing. On the other side rose the mountain itself.

Was that the toll house?

The air felt drier on that side of the bridge. And much colder. Christine shivered and stepped back from the eastern edge, away from the wall there, shaking her head.

The view was replaced with more meadow and trees, the night softer, warmer. It matched the western view, now.

This *was* a portal to the other lands. Christine hadn't thought Joe was lying, but it was exciting to see it for herself.

Did Nikolai know about this bridge? Did Ty? Of course they did. Had they, too, just assumed that she already knew about it?

Or was Joe wrong, and were there portals that could be used to get in and out of the lands of the *kith and kin*?

It made sense that they'd be forbidden.

It also made sense that demons and other types would have found a way around those rules.

With a heavy sigh, Christine turned back around, facing west. Facing the rest of Seattle. Her human home.

She did *not* want to break this bridge. She pushed down at the clawing need inside her. Could she wait? Could she maybe go explore, first? At least warn the people in the toll house what was coming?

The fire elemental inside her surged up impatiently. Without meaning to, Christine blasted the stone wall to the west with angry blue flames.

The wall lit up in response. The same sigil that had

been at the other two sites burned brightly at the heart of each stone that Christine had touched with her flame.

At least Christine knew this was the right place.

She struggled to push the fire elemental down, to soothe it. Water came bubbling up in response, like a jealous dog, wanting attention as well.

Christine tried to placate the elementals inside of her while the sigil before her grew brighter. Larger.

Stones cracked ominously under her feet as the bright light burned.

Damn it! She needed to pay attention to what was happening right before her. And not just what was inside her head.

She gave a contemptuous snort at that. Hadn't Dennis said that to her more than once?

She'd have to remember to tell him about it later.

The bridge rumbled as the stones under her feet shifted ominously.

If she survived.

As with the fire elemental, Christine didn't have to push herself forward. The air elemental already knew her, knew she was there. At first, the sigil of blue light, that skewed treble clef, had only been on the stone wall. Now, it spread. Each stone along the base of the bridge now spouted smaller versions of the same sign. Replicas raced across the footpath, to the other wall, the lights springing up.

Christine would have thought it was pretty, the bridge

lit with magical blue light, if the winds hadn't started racing out of the center of each of the sigils.

Christine had imagined that there would be a single air elemental or wind for her to fight and tame.

Instead, there were myriad little winds that pushed and pulled at her, stinging blows striking her face, arms, legs—anywhere they could reach.

This wasn't a grand enemy, but the death of a thousand cuts.

What would appease the winds? Christine cupped her hand and offered some of her fire but the winds knocked her hand away, scattering the sparks. She quickly doused her light. She didn't want to set the entire park on fire.

She couldn't call up water, make it just appear in her hands, though she suspected the winds would be just as contemptuous of that.

These winds felt aloof, above all things earth-bound. They didn't care about her or anything she could offer.

They just wanted to be free to fly around the world. They had mischief on their minds. Old branches to crack. Cars to send skidding. Puddles to splash and skirts to lift.

As well as darker tricks. Ocean waves to whip into a frenzy. Ships to topple over and sink. Roofs to blow off. Mountaineers to pluck from their lines.

A trail of fire trickled from Christine's fingertips. Before she could call it back, she noticed one of the winds circling around it.

Christine drew circles in the air with her finger. The fire turned into a thin rope. It encircled the small wind, drew it toward her.

When the wind seeped into Christine's skin, she

couldn't help her shiver. It was cold and wild and uncaring. While she felt as though she could relate to her fire and water elementals, her air elemental seemed foreign to her.

Still, she recognized it as part of her that had been missing. There were empty sockets under her skin that only the winds could fill.

She'd have to worry about integrating them later. Worry about how she would change, or not. After she'd captured the winds.

Christine sent out more thin tendrils of fire, looping them around, from both her right and left hands. She captured more tiny winds that way, little whirlwinds dancing in the air like dust devils, sparkling with blue light before giving her skin a stinging kiss and sliding inside her.

Christine couldn't tell if she was winning or not. There were so many small winds! Her stomach suddenly churned, as if she was about to vomit. She was full. Overly full.

And there were more winds.

Were some getting away? She couldn't tell. She'd never be able to count them all.

The bridge under her feet suddenly shifted again.

Christine looked up and gasped. She'd been too focused on the little winds.

But those didn't make up the entirety of her air elemental.

No, they'd just been a distraction.

A much larger whirlwind rose up before her, cracking the stones of the bridge apart.

This was her true power. This mini-tornado, whirling and angry, cackling with power, lightning streaking inside it, full of sparking blue lights.

It swirled past her contemptuously, banging into first one wall of the bridge, then the other, deliberately tearing them down, sending the stones flying.

"No! Stop!" Christine shouted.

The wind ignored her. More rocks went flying, this time directly at Christine.

Christine shook her hands, ridding herself of the smaller ropes.

This wind wanted to play rough?

Bring it.

Christine called up a greater fire in her hands, planning on braiding it into a larger rope. She was going to lasso this wind elemental. Hog-tie it and bring it to the ground.

The wind elemental realized what she was doing. It stopped destroying the walls of the bridge and bounced directly in front of Christine. It dropped heavily onto the stones there, then whirled with a purpose.

Before Christine could finish forming the rope, the bridge gave a final *crack* that echoed deep in Christine's bones.

She found herself falling.

At least it wasn't too far to the ground.

Before she reached it, though, her wind elemental grabbed her and floated her up.

Christine was suddenly at the same height she'd been before, as high as the now broken bridge, held up by unseen hands.

Casually, without malice, her air elemental started sucking all the air into itself.

Sucking away all the air away from Christine.

She couldn't breathe.

~

Christine struggled to get away. She imagined she must be quite a sight to Ty and Joe—floating in mid-air, pushing, pulling, frantically kicking, trying to free herself. A demon of wind whirled before her, the blue lights cold and malicious. She couldn't smell anything but snow and cold iron, couldn't hear anything but the great roar of the gale.

"Let me go!" Christine commanded.

The wind laughed at her. "Why? So you can capture me? Bind me again?"

"You're a part of me!" Christine told it firmly.

Black spots were already forming in front of her eyes.

"And you abandoned me," the wind accused her.

"I did not!" Christine protested. Fire sprang up all around her. Was it trying to save her? Save itself?

Or trying to tear itself loose as well?

"You were stolen from me," Christine managed to croak out. "Demons…demons took you."

She didn't know if that was true or not. But demons had bound her other elements. It seemed only right.

Her head pounded and felt as if it would explode. The fire burned her skin.

She was powerful, yes. But she had no idea how to use that power, or what to do with it.

"You're part demon, you know," the wind said maliciously.

Christine stubbornly shook her head, trying to save her breath.

She tried to rally the fire around her, to make it heed her. Tried to fashion the rope again to lasso the wind and draw it toward her. Her fingers felt swollen and clumsy. Her tongue, too, was bulging in her throat.

She needed air. And soon.

Surprisingly, her water elemental fizzed up inside her. There wasn't a lot of oxygen in it. But it carried air bubbles to her, popping them inside her. It was an unsettling feeling, all those bubbles bursting at once. Like sparks sizzling under her skin.

But Christine's head cleared. She had a little more time before she choked to death.

She fashioned the rope quickly and cast it out toward the whirling wind.

The mini-tornado stood where it was, letting itself be captured.

Now what?

Christine tugged on the wind, but she couldn't draw it to her. She had nothing to ground herself, nothing to tug against. The wind still held her in midair. Helpless.

"What do you want?" Christine called out, desperate. Her air elemental seemed much more aware than either of the other elements, much more of a separate being. Had much more will, too. Was that because it had been part of a magical bridge?

Though she suspected her fire elemental would never

fully integrate either—that it would always test her and its bounds.

Was that natural? Or had the demons who had bound her power tainted them, somehow?

"Ah," the wind crooned. "I want a favor."

"What?" Christine asked, hesitant. What kind of favor would a wind elemental ask for? She suspected it was even more tricksy than the fire elemental.

"A promise of a future favor, nothing more," the wind sighed.

"I can't give you that," Christine said stubbornly. "You might ask me to kill someone. Or do something that was wrong. Or even ask to be freed."

She might not be breathing well, and she might *need* this elemental, but she wasn't about to promise to do something dishonorable.

Her mother would never let her hear the end of it.

The wind laughed at her. Again. "No, silly. I'll be a part of you. I won't be able to ask you something that you wouldn't already consider doing yourself."

Christine still hesitated. Her troll self was more prone to violence than her human self. She already knew that.

Did she trust this creature to stay within the bounds of a promise?

"It won't be anything bad?" Christine asked, weakening.

"Evil, like beauty, is in the eye of the beholder," the wind told her.

It did draw closer, though. Christine pulled the slack up from her fire lasso, though she knew it wasn't actually holding the wind there.

"Come, child. Make up your mind. Do you want my power with you? Or to die alone? Without knowing your true Destiny?"

"I don't have a Destiny," Christine complained. Tina had been the one with a Destiny. Not her.

Or had the Zimmermans been lying about that as well?

"Promise me a future promise," the wind said sharply. It tugged away a little.

"I promise," Christine said. The words rang out again, as she'd known they would. "But only if you keep your word as well."

The wind laughed again, merrily for once.

"Oh, I will. I promise."

It wasn't bell-like tones that followed the wind's words, but a tinkling sound, like metal chimes brushed lightly.

And with that, the wind bounced closer, brushing against Christine's burning skin, quenching her fire, calming her water.

The wind *knew* so many things, whispering them to her as it whirled around her. About the old king of Trollville, sitting all alone on his throne, his children gone. About the Great War still looming, the demon armies massing in pocket worlds hidden between the real worlds. About the Host and how the court's hands were tied.

Of evil and power land good and bad.

Christine gasped, trying to draw it all in. She felt as though she couldn't breathe again, too much wind stealing her breath away, too many ideas whirling in her brain, too much power itching and restless under her skin.

Finally, though, the wind was done, making a home

inside of her. Christine felt bloated. She was afraid if she bent over she'd vomit up everything inside of her.

She was also, still, floating in mid-air. No ground under her feet to hold her steady. She felt herself tipping to one side, and with an effort righted herself. Then she willed herself to the earth, her feet stumbling on the broken stones. She felt their anguish for a moment before the magic slipped completely out of them and they grew mute.

That was wrong. These stones should sing. She knew they could, when they were properly aligned, fulfilling their purpose.

Christine looked up. The edges of the bridge were like jagged, broken teeth in the air. She mourned the loss of the bridge. It had stood for ages, she now knew. Long before the first man had crossed these woods, seeking berries and smaller prey.

She knelt gingerly and patted one of the stones. She *would* rebuild the bridge. Heal the rocks, patch their wounds.

She'd promised.

CHAPTER 7

Christine lurched into Nikolai's shop later the next evening. Just the thought of staying home had left her nauseated, her head spinning.

She couldn't stop moving. Couldn't stop humming under her breath. Couldn't stop muttering as the powers inside her squabbled, though mainly she found herself saying, "Stop that!"

Her co-workers were really starting to worry about her.

So was she, if she was honest with herself.

She couldn't eat anything—felt full beyond reckoning. And despite needing to move, she still had to be cautious. Was afraid that bending over or moving too quickly and she'd end up vomiting. Again.

She wasn't drunk with power. That had only happened the first time, with her water power—the joy, the ease.

Air should be light, right? Yet Christine felt weighted, ponderous, slow and old. All the noise of the powers inside her made her head pound. Her jaw ached from clenching it. She hadn't slept well, either.

She was almost tempted to try something alcoholic, just to get the elementals to shut up and give her some peace.

How was she supposed to work with them bickering this way? How could she do anything at all? When she'd tried to raise a small light she'd nearly scorched her apartment ceiling. The next time, the light had been the size of a pea in her palm and she couldn't get it to grow in the least.

So despite how ill she felt, she knew she needed some help. Hence, her trip to Nikolai's magical emporium.

The shop still looked the same, the same cheery lights, the shelves still filled with kits for making charms, ingredients for charms, potions, and spells, plus a much expanded section of books (though Nikolai had been right and they hadn't sold that well). Flashy posters advertising the more expensive magical goods hung above the shelves.

There were differences, too. The posters—some of them sparkled, now. More of the shelves had a shimmer to them, too. Like the velvet, silk, and burlap bags for holding charms. She'd always thought they were plain cloth. Did they already have spells cast on them? Christine hadn't seen it before. The powders, in their carefully sealed jars, also glowed with a dull haze.

It would make sense that she could see magical things better, now that she, herself, was more magical.

However, trying to concentrate on any one thing made her head pound worse.

Nikolai was helping a customer up front—a brownie,

as far as Christine could tell. He was ugly, with boils all over his face and dark, harsh lines under his eyes. His long-sleeved shirt made of black denim and his knee-length breaches were neat and clean, and his black leather clogs shone.

"What are you looking at?" he challenged Christine as she came up to the counter.

Christine bristled. How dare he challenge her? She belonged here, more than he did.

Then she shook her head. No, no, Nik's place was neutral. She'd get banned for fighting.

"I'm not looking at anything," Christine growled quietly at him. She didn't give him another look though she could well imagine the shock on his face when she slipped behind the counter and went through the blue velvet curtains to the back room.

The lights there were too bright. The good smell of earth was gone. The tall bookcases and scent of dry ink didn't comfort her as usual. The boxes here, too, pulsed with a magic that pushed at her, making her feel queasy.

Christine paced from one end of the room to the other, too agitated to try to make sense of anything.

She needed help. Desperately.

"You've been finding your powers," Nikolai said as soon as he walked into the room.

Christine merely nodded. She assumed she looked as bloated as she felt.

"Demons bound them," she said darkly. If she ever got her hands on Lars… She wasn't sure exactly what she would do. But it wouldn't be pretty.

Even the laughing wind inside her agreed.

"Are you sure?" Nikolai asked.

Christine got out her phone and showed him the pictures she'd taken of the graffiti from the first two sites. It hadn't shown up on the bridge. She wasn't sure why, or what that meant.

Then again, her wind had been bound to every stone in the bridge. It had been a much more complete binding than the others.

Nikolai gave a low whistle. "That's high magic," he said slowly. "Not casual. Those types of spells can only be cast after months of preparation."

"Who would do such a thing?" Christine asked. She bit her tongue before she asked the next question: Had Nikolai sold the ingredients for the spells?

Nikolai shook his head. "Not a clue. But I would bet someone at the local court would know."

Christine sighed. She didn't want to have to go to the courthouse again. She was already eating up her sick days as it was. Maybe she could just take a long lunch break…

"You know the damage you've done has been in the news," Nikolai said.

Christine shrugged. She felt bad about that. But there hadn't been anything she could do about it.

"The old fire station was vandalized," Nikolai continued. "Rooms destroyed inside of it."

Christine paused. "Wait. All I did was call my water elemental from the outside. Only the front wall should have been damaged."

"That's not what was shown on the news. It looks like someone took an ax to the walls in the front hall. Broke pipes and flooded the place."

Christine shook her head, then stopped, the motion making her dizzy. "It wasn't me."

"Breaking the binding may have set off other spells," Nikolai said. "Caused the rest of the damage. So it *would* be in the news. That way, whoever took your powers would know for certain that you were getting them back. A backup, in case you circumvented any warning spells that had been set up."

Christine shivered. This demon really had it in for her.

She told Nikolai about the visitation from Lars, how he'd said it was part of a feud between his family and another demon's.

Nikolai nodded. "That makes sense. I'd volunteer to look into it, but the feuds between the demon houses are more convoluted than a Mexican soap opera. First they're friends, then they're sworn enemies, then they have a deal, then one side breaks it and the other sues them—it's just a mess."

Christine looked at Nikolai, blinking away tears that she hadn't realized were so close. "So am I," she whispered. She didn't know if she was coming or going, didn't know what was her or her powers'. Couldn't get a handle on anything.

The little wooden man gave her a tight smile. "Let's see what we can do to put you to rights then."

He held out his wooden hand to her. All the joints were perfectly articulated. Though his hand was tiny in her palm, it still felt warm and strong.

A portal appeared, blue and swirling.

Christine stiffened. Where was Nikolai taking her? Did she trust him?

Did she have a choice?

With a deep gulp of air, Christine took a step forward.

Again, the rallying cry.

Here goes nothing.

~

Heat blasted Christine as she stumbled through the portal. Her head was still spinning. The rough dirt beneath her feet grated against her skin. The smell of smoke burned her nose, thick and oily, though she couldn't see any—the sky was a clear blue above miles and miles of barren rock.

They stood on a steep slope. The rocks were gray and bleached, like bones. Christine turned to look up the hill. Fog covered the peak. Winds stirred it. Shapes of large creatures formed inside the mist, then vanished.

Christine shivered despite the heat. This was a very magical pocket world. She'd generally associated magic with a sweeter smell, but here, she could taste it, far back in her throat, acrid and bitter.

The powers inside her had at least subsided. For the moment. They felt uneasy in this place. But they'd at least stopped bickering.

Was Nikolai taller here? Maybe instead of being three feet tall he was three feet, two inches. He did look thinner, the features on his face appearing more cartoony. His, well, skin, had a much paler sheen to it, as though he was constructed of birch instead of golden maple.

"There's nothing here that you can hurt," Nikolai told her as he walked closer to her.

It was odd how his mouth moved here—his wooden lips actually moving across his face instead of his mouth just hinging open and closed.

"Even that mist?" Christine asked, waving uphill.

How did Nikolai appear to squint when his eyes were merely painted on? Christine had never been able to figure that out.

"It will leave us alone as long as we leave it alone," he said after a moment. "So come." Nikolai started walking down the hill.

Christine didn't want to turn her back on the mist, but she did, following after the little wooden man.

He led them to a more level area. Huge boulders lay flattened against the hill, as if some great hand had smashed them into the earth. A cold wind blew between them, moaning.

Nikolai stood to one side and directed Christine to face downhill. "Now, bring up a light," he said.

Christine raised her hand. She gave a great sigh of relief when a normal light appeared in her palm, not some great fireball.

"What power is working with you to do that?" Nikolai asked.

Christine pondered. She'd been able to bring up a light after she'd gotten her water power. But light wasn't necessarily a part of the water elemental.

"None of them," she said after a moment. "I think it's just me." Her squabbling powers were still quiescent inside of her. Not that they were bound or something, or couldn't act. She had a sense that they were waiting. For what, she wasn't sure.

"Good, good!" Nikolai said. "You're starting to find your true essence."

That made Christine feel better. Did that mean that her water power had integrated when she'd absorbed it? It had certainly felt that way.

Would she be able to do the same with the other two?

"Can you change the color of the light?" Nikolai asked.

Christine focused on the small light in her hands. It was easy enough to shift it to a darker blue color. Could she make it glow red?

The light changed to a bright yellow, then with a mighty *woof* transformed into a huge fireball.

Alarmed, Christine tried to pull her fire elemental back.

It was having nothing to do with her caution, though. The ball of flame gleefully leaped from her hand onto the rocks. It danced there a few minutes, mocking her, before she was able to extinguish it.

"I see," Nikolai said. "Your natural ability should allow you to make colored lights—many different colored lights."

"Like jewels," Christine said. She remembered her daydream of the tunnels leading off from her apartment, with shining jewels in the wall, *in situ*. There had been lights as well, just as colorful.

"I hadn't thought of the colored lights like that, but yes, exactly," Nikolai said. "You know I've never worked with a magical troll before, right?"

Christine nodded. "I remember." There weren't many

trolls. Now, there would be even fewer, since she'd broken the bridge.

"Did you know about the bridge to Trollville?" she asked suddenly.

"Yes and no," the wooden man said, tilting his head from side to side. "It's a well-known secret that there are paths to the other worlds. Many of the worlds are blocked off from portals. As I'm not really *kith and kin*, I couldn't officially know."

Was that why Ty hadn't said anything? He wasn't really *kith and kin* either.

"What *are* you?" Christine couldn't help but ask. She'd known at some level that Nikolai wasn't the same as her, but she still wasn't sure what exactly he was.

Nikolai gave her a great grin. "I'm a made man," he said proudly. "One of a kind. An artifact, imbued with life."

"I see," Christine said, though she didn't. Not really. But what had she expected? He looked like a wooden man. She did find she was a bit disappointed, though, that there wasn't a whole tribe of wooden people, somewhere.

"Because of who I am, how I was created, I can stay truly neutral during the wars," Nikolai added.

Christine remembered the news the air elemental had carried as it sank into her, about the demon armies amassing. "The Great War is still coming, isn't it," she asked flatly.

"It is. And because you've broken the bridge, you may have aided the side of the demons," he said.

"What?" Christine asked, shocked.

Nikolai gave a stiff, wooden-man shrug. The

appearance of his shoulders going up and down unsettled Christine. "The *kith and kin* will want to leave their lands. Travel. They're going to have to relax some of the strictures on portals."

"So they'll be open for attack. Because of me," Christine said bitterly. Why couldn't she have waited? At least until she'd found her earth power first?

She was really going to tear into Lars the next time he appeared.

"Wait. Stop," Nikolai said.

Christine looked at him, puzzled. She hadn't been going anywhere.

"No one, not even the court and all the angels, can avoid all the traps the demons set. Before you spiral into a morass of blame and self-doubt, know that you're stronger than they expected you to be. I bet they figured you'd fail."

Christine nodded slowly. Lars did expect her to fail. To die, without her powers. To just blow up the bridge and not come after him.

"Let's prove them wrong," Christine said after another moment.

She *was* going to replace that bridge. She just had to find her earth power.

And figure out how to use all her magic for good.

Unfortunately, Christine stating that she wanted to learn how to use her magic, and being willing to practice, and actually being successful at doing magic, were completely different things.

The gray rocks on the hill they stood on in the pocket world held great scorch marks and gashes from when Christine had lost control of her power. Again and again. Some of the rocks lay smashed and splintered, from when her air elemental had gotten bored with lifting a rock and had just dropped it. Or had spitefully flung it.

Christine had been excited when her water elemental had managed to raise a trickle of water from underneath the stones—only to have it turn foul, brackish, and possibly poisonous.

Nikolai was frustrated as well. Though he didn't have human shoulders, Christine could tell they were stiff, tense.

She could do a little bit with her own powers. She'd discovered that she could change her appearance to anything she imagined. A useful skill, though a touch unnerving. Particularly when she'd managed to make herself into a perfect wooden doll, a female replica of Nikolai.

The shopkeeper had found that as disturbing as she had, and she'd changed back into her troll form quickly.

She didn't know what she was doing wrong. How to integrate the various part of herself. Using magic didn't seem to be helping: If anything, her elementals were fighting with each other even more now, trying to prove themselves the best or the strongest or something equally stupid.

Christine had never wanted children. Now, more than ever. Her powers constantly arguing made it feel as if she had three teenagers living inside her.

She felt a bit more sympathy and understanding for

her parents, how they'd put up with her and Dennis fighting all the time when they'd been younger.

Nikolai had asked her to try various things, with varying degrees of success. She couldn't make a rock turn invisible, but when Nikolai had, she'd still been able to see it. Ditto when he'd "twinned" a rock, creating an illusion of a second, identical stone standing next to the original.

Christine had always been able to tell which one was the duplicate. Not by sight, but by some feeling, deep inside her.

It made her feel better that she was naturally able to see through some level of illusions.

"Okay, let's try one last thing, then I think we both deserve some hot chocolate. Or a stiff whisky," Nikolai finally said.

Christine wasn't certain how the made man would ingest food. She'd never seen him eat or drink anything. She was tired though, and not about to turn down his suggestion.

"Or?" she asked, teasing.

"You're right. Hot chocolate AND whisky." Nikolai gave her a sly grin. "Now, I want you to try to form fog."

"Fog?" Christine asked, puzzled.

"Try either a pool of fog, or maybe a wall of fog," Nikolai instructed. "That would get your air and water elementals to work together."

"Okay," Christine said.

She held out her hands and asked, one last time, for her elementals to cooperate. She felt the fog inside her already. It was cool, like the Seattle rain in the fall. Misty.

It made her feel good. This was part of her home. She could bring it here.

The fog poured out of her hands, billowing across the open plain. It started as thin mist, a dim shroud over everything, then coalesced into a fog, obscuring all the rocks.

"Like that?" Christine asked Nikolai with a grin.

"Not quite," he said. He sounded worried. "We need to go. Now."

Christine dropped her hands. Dismissed the fog.

The fog didn't dissipate in the least.

"What's wrong?" she asked.

Nikolai raised his hands, fingers spread wide. He arched them out, then down.

Nothing happened.

Nikolai frowned and very deliberately mimed the outline of a portal.

Nothing sprang up. No blue lights. No swirling mass of magic.

"What's wrong?" Christine asked again.

"Your fog. It challenged the fog on the hill," Nikolai said with a grimace.

"I didn't mean to…" Christine said. In fact, she wasn't sure how she'd done it.

Had one of her powers imbued her fog with extra talents? That wouldn't surprise her.

It hadn't been her air power, either, but her water elemental, trying to prove her worth to Christine.

Damn it! How could Christine control them better?

The mist that billowed in front of Christine and Nik changed. Christine could tell that it was being taken over by the fog native to this place, the scent of Seattle rain changing to smoke again, that burnt oil smell.

Figures formed in the fog. Creatures that Christine really didn't want to have to fight—winged and horned and scaled things from her nightmares.

Nikolai was muttering spells to himself, drawing his own bright, shining light into his hands, trying to dispel the quickly gathering fog.

Christine determinedly called up her air power. *You think you're so great. Do your thing,* she challenged.

The little winds came at first, tentative. Christine cast them into the fog where they swirled around, undoing first a claw, then a leg, leaving the creatures hobbled.

Nikolai suddenly spoke up. "Good. Keep them distracted for another few minutes and I'll be able to get us out of here."

Something about his tone, about how he assumed all she could be was a distraction, rankled Christine. Her back stiffened and her hands formed automatically into claws.

She made herself take a deep breath, telling herself to calm down.

Nikolai had been nothing but helpful. She shouldn't be angry with him.

She'd still show him. Merely a distraction, huh?

Great gusts of wind suddenly blasted the wall of fog before them, pushing it back.

That seemed to surprise the fog. It surged toward them again, valiantly.

Christine's fire elemental came into play. She cast great bolts of light through the darkness, the winds pushing it back, her water elemental sucking all the life away from the foreign fog.

Christine wasn't satisfied with the fog merely pulling away, though. She stomped on the ground, causing the rock beneath her to splint. A cloud of dirt and dust rose up that Christine used her winds to gleefully cast into the fog.

Christine might not have her earth elemental back, but she still had an affinity for good stone and dirt.

This fog was of this place, this land of heat and stone. Christine couldn't destroy it, not without killing the pocket world itself.

She could drive it back, though. It was a creature of the air. She could infect it with the ground. Bind it to the rock.

The great rush of anger Christine felt as she lashed at the fog shook her to her core. She tried to pull back, to get her powers under control again.

This fog had tried to stop them from leaving, yes, but she didn't have to completely destroy it. Did she?

When Christine looked up, she saw Nikolai staring at her with a peculiar expression on his face, one she couldn't read. Disgust? Admiration? A combination of both?

The fog had pulled back a respectful distance. It boiled there, glowering at them.

It would permit them to leave. This time.

It wasn't about to admit that it didn't have a choice, that Christine had almost destroyed it, that it was, in some way, scared and ashamed of its fear.

"I'm not sure I want to know what you did," Nikolai

said as he sketched the portal opening. It sprang up, a welcome, blue swirling light. "But I'm glad you did it."

~

Later that night, sitting in her living room, the book in her hands failing to interest her, Christine wondered about the same things—how evil might be in the eye of the beholder, how she might have advanced the war, how she was going to rebuild the bridge, and how she was going to continue.

She knew she needed to find her earth power, and soon. She'd never be fully herself until she did. The other powers inside her needed something to anchor them. She could only assume that part of why she felt so out of balance was because she didn't have her earth power yet.

What if she didn't like who she turned out to be? came a niggling voice from somewhere deep inside her. That rush of anger from that afternoon still bothered her. How she'd almost destroyed the native fog in that pocket world. Or bound it, as her powers had been bound.

But she wasn't fully herself, or who she was supposed to be. Not yet. Not until after she found her earth power.

And as Dennis had frequently said—she'd burn that bridge when she came to it.

CHAPTER 8

Christine dragged herself to her job the next day. She'd taken off a day and a half already. Though she had more sick days accumulated, she didn't want to spend them all.

Besides, just sitting in her apartment with all her powers fizzing and snapping at her and each other wasn't any fun.

Normally, Christine loved being in the archives of the library. The rich smell of history. The dry ink. The fragile papers with all that lovely knowledge.

Today, she found herself impatient with everything. She had to bite her tongue to stop herself from snapping at one of the other librarians. She nearly roared with displeasure when she found some of the old maps had been misfiled.

Finally, she couldn't take it anymore and clocked out early for lunch, stomping up to the street.

Of course, it was hotter than hell out there. The

archives were at least kept at a reasonable temperature, to preserve the delicate artifacts stored there.

Christine was already sweating as she made her way up the street. No one smiled or said hello to her that day— they all looked away, not making eye contact.

Not engaging the crazy person.

Christine paused when she reached the street corner. She didn't know where she was going, what she was doing, what she wanted.

Then she realized that she'd left her packed lunch back in the fridge in the break room.

She'd just eat it later. Growling, she picked a direction, going with the first green light, down Fourth.

"Aren't you a little early?" came a voice that sounded as sullen as she felt.

Christine stopped.

Lars stood there, smugly leaning against the wall of an office building.

With a great roar, Christine *slammed* her fist through his face, into the wall.

It didn't hurt him. Of course. He was just a projection.

The look of shock and surprise on his face still made her hurt knuckles worth it.

"Go away," Christine told him curtly. "I don't need your help."

Lars' eyes grew big as he took her in. "I can see that. You have, what, two? Three? Of your powers already?"

"Three," Christine said smugly. "No help from you."

"No, I think it's all due to my help," Lars said with a grin. "I told you where to find the first one."

"All right. Fine," Christine admitted. "Now be on your way."

"I can't do that, not in good conscience," Lars said with fake concern. "I need to warn you about the error of your ways."

"You know, when you get out of prison, there won't be anything to stop me from ripping your balls off and feeding them to you," Christine growled at him.

Lars rolled his eyes at her threat.

So he wasn't afraid of a physical confrontation? Fine.

"Then I'll have your ass thrown back in jail for continuing to harass me. I'll bring up more charges, too, that it was your idea to break the artifacts that my powers were bound to. That you *encouraged* me, in fact, to commit vandalism."

Lars managed to pale at that. Impressive, given how pasty white his skin already was. "It'll never stick."

"Try me," Christine promised him. "You can protest all you want, but a judge is never going to believe you."

"You'll be joining me here, though," Lars told her fiercely. "For all the known damage you've done. For *destroying* the bridge."

"I'll rebuild the bridge," Christine told him nonchalantly. "Once I get my earth power back. You wouldn't happen to know where that was bound, would you?"

Lars pressed his lips together tightly and shook his head. "I can't tell you," he said prissily. "Do you know what you're doing, by breaking the bindings of your powers so completely?"

"Why don't you tell me," Christine dared him. "And

remember, with my powers, now, I can tell when you're lying."

A fleeting look of worry crossed Lars' face before he brazened on. "You remember I told you that it was Ming the Merciless who had bound your powers?"

Christine realized to her horror that Lars *had* told her that. And that the name would mean nothing to her. She'd meant to ask Ty about it, but she'd forgotten in the rush of everything else. "I remember," she said, a little deflated.

"Ming is binder for the court. For the Host," Lars said. "Once you break all your bindings, every case that Ming has ever worked on will need to be reexamined. Many of those bindings of his will have to be reworked by someone more competent."

Christine understood immediately. "Like your case. And whatever it is that keeps you bound in prison," she guessed.

"Exactly!" Lars exclaimed. "And we should be able to find someone much more amenable to our situation."

"Let's see. You'll find someone you can bribe. So you'll merely be under house arrest or something, and not in actual jail."

Which meant that Lars would be free to continue his schemes and plans, that his family would be free to restart the Great War.

"You really are smarter than you look," Lars commented.

Christine narrowed her eyes at him, though she knew that her glare would be just as ineffective as her fist had been.

"So are you going to stop searching for your powers? Breaking the bindings?" Lars asked gleefully.

Christine knew better than to lie to him. He'd spot a lie more quickly than she would, as he lived and breathed them. "You've given me a lot to think about," she told him truthfully.

That was neither a yes nor a no.

Lars seemed a little deflated at that.

Christine took a step back. She felt a tiny bit more settled now that she'd had the chance to hurt Lars.

She didn't necessarily like what that said about her. But she couldn't worry about it now.

"I think play time is over," she told him firmly. "You need to get your ass back in jail. Go. Now."

Christine didn't think she actually had any power over Lars, that he'd actually heed her words.

But he started fading as soon as she told him to leave.

Of course, the asshole had to get the last word in.

"Remember, you've been warned! Consider your actions!"

Christine sighed and grumbled to herself as she started back the way she'd come, up the street and toward the library.

He was right. She didn't want him freed. And what other creatures had this Ming the Merciless bound? What sort of terror would she be releasing on the human world, as well as the various lands of the *kith and kin,* if all his bindings were called into question?

Did it matter if the bindings of her own power were illegal? Done against her will? Did one wrong make that right?

Christine knew she couldn't answer those questions, not for herself, not yet. These types of arguments always made her head hurt, anyway.

Mum and Dad had raised her to do the right thing.

The problem was, what was right?

~

As soon as Christine got her next break, she called Ty. He didn't answer. Must be on a case. She left him a terse message, asking that he call her back immediately.

She had only just put her phone down and picked up the Library Chronicles newsletter when her phone buzzed.

"What's up?" Ty asked brusquely.

"Who's Ming the Merciless?" Christine asked, aiming for innocence, not sure she hit the mark.

"I take it you don't mean the movie character," Ty said after a moment. He huffed, then a clattering noise came over the phone.

"What are you doing?" Christine asked.

"Running for my life," Ty told her cheerfully.

"Then why are you calling me?" Christine asked, exasperated. Really, didn't he know any better?

"You know me. I like the challenge. If I make it out alive, I'll see you later tonight," Ty said. "Ow!"

The phone went dead.

First of all, Christine was impressed that he'd managed to call. He had to be someplace here on earth, because phones didn't work in the other worlds.

Would he be all right? There wasn't much she could do if he wasn't, except maybe to enact some revenge.

Christine took a deep breath and tried to settle herself back down.

Her phone buzzed again.

This time, it was Dennis.

"So I know you've been avoiding me," Dennis started off.

"Hello, Dennis, how are you?" Christine said pointedly. "Why, I'm fine, thank you for asking."

She didn't have to see him to know how hard he was rolling his eyes right now.

"All right. Sorry." He took a breath and continued. "I take it that you're the one who's been wrecking things around Capitol Hill the last few nights?"

"Guilty as charged," Christine told him. After an awkward pause, she added, "I was going to call you."

"You know, I'm not sure I believe you, this time," Dennis said. "Guess who came to pay me a little visit?"

Oh jeez. "Lars," Christine said. She shook her head. Handing him his balls was going to be just the start of the punishment she'd inflict on him once she had her hands on him—

"How do you—oh. He came to see you too, right?" Dennis asked.

"Yeah. He came to visit me. Told me about the first elemental. Remember?" Christine said, puzzled. Had Dennis forgotten?

"Oh. Right. Yeah," Dennis said. "Well, he just told me he'd come to see you a second time. And that what you were doing was wrong."

Christine sighed. She so didn't want to be having this conversation on the phone. "Yeah, he came to see me. And yes, he told me that I needed to stop. And why. This was why I was going to call you. So I could talk with you." She paused, then added, "And maybe Mum and Dad as well."

Christine had never heard shocked silence before.

"Really?" he asked, his voice full of wonder.

"Yes," Christine said. Then she realized what had happened. "Lars told you that I was going to do something different, didn't he?"

A small guilty voice replied. "Yes?"

Now it was Christine's opportunity to roll her eyes. "And you believed him?"

"You've been avoiding me!" Dennis accused her. "Dodging my calls. And you have changed, you know. Since this spring."

Christine nodded. She understood. She really did. Her human family didn't get her at all, not as a troll, no matter how much they tried to be supportive.

"I know," Christine said. The elementals inside her stirred up briefly, wanting to flee, wanting to burn, wanting to rain down pain on them all.

Just as quickly, the feelings subsided. This was her family, after all.

They'd always made her kind of crazy.

"Want to meet for tacos and drinks tonight?" Christine asked. "On the deck."

They'd had many family meetings on the deck while Christine had been growing up. It was going to be beastly hot, but at least they'd be outside. There was a chance of some kind of breeze coming from Lake Washington.

Maybe Christine would be able to sit and be calm for a short while.

"You're on," Dennis said. "I'll call Mum and Dad. You bring the tacos."

"See you later, then," Christine said. She nearly asked him to come and pick her up, then thought better of it.

It would be better if she could get there on her own. Prove that she was still capable, and not the wild, willful creature that Lars had probably very effectively drawn for Dennis, playing on his fears.

Really, if she ever got her claws on that demon…she didn't actually know what she'd do.

If destroying him was what her air power asked her to do, that future favor she still owed, would she say no?

Christine cursed silently as she stepped off the (second!) dead bus and into the blistering heat of the afternoon. The sun beat down mercilessly. The other passengers grumbled as well as they walked down the block, across the street, and toward the inadequate bus shelter. A long line of cars crawled past the dead bus, stretching back for blocks. Probably miles.

Damn it! When would another bus make it through that traffic? In an hour? Two?

The first bus Christine had gotten on had only made it a few blocks past downtown before it had died. It had lowered its front step to let on someone in a wheelchair. But the driver had lowered the step too far. It had gotten stuck, with the step grating on the concrete curb, unable to raise back up.

The second bus had just stalled out and couldn't be restarted about halfway up a hill, in the Madison Valley neighborhood.

Just down a bit and across the street stood the Arboretum.

A spike of fear ran through Christine as she paused on the sidewalk.

Would someone recognize her as the one who'd destroyed the footbridge there?

But no one seemed to be looking at her. They all had their own misery.

Christine heaved a sigh as she started walking toward the stoplight. It was too far to walk to her parents' house. The bag of tacos was heavy in her hand, the grease dripping through and already staining the white plastic bag. She wore a cute black skirt and a lightweight, sleeveless, lavender blouse, but she'd sweated through all of it when she'd stepped out of the library over an hour ago.

She could call a cab—probably half of the other passengers who'd stopped at the corner and were now staring at their phones were doing just that. But it would cost too much. She'd already dipped into her savings earlier that spring when the changeling spell had first broken, buying magical supplies and protection charms. She hadn't really been able to build her nest egg back up.

Plus, given the traffic, and the number of people waiting, who knew when a taxi would actually arrive?

Christine had been avoiding activating a portal and

then using it. She wasn't sure what would happen since her powers were so out of control.

But she was already late for dinner with her parents.

Maybe she should call Dennis? Have him come and get her? He'd understand if the bus had broken down. Twice.

No. He'd bitch the entire way about the traffic. And she wasn't going to rely on him. She could solve this problem on her own.

Christine marched deliberately across the street and down along the road into the park. Lovely trees arched overhead. The shade was nice, though it barely made a difference given the heat. She could tell the trees were distressed from the lack of water, but they valiantly held their branches high. A constant stream of cars passed by in both directions. Joggers filled the sidewalk, along with people walking their dogs.

Why anyone would voluntarily exercise in this heat was beyond Christine. Most of the people she passed didn't have a smile for her—they were all grimacing, as if on a death march.

Christine couldn't smell the earth or the trees—wisps of smoke still filled her senses. She still felt bloated. Why couldn't her water power at least cool her off? Or her wind power? But no. They had to squabble and fight instead of helping her out.

It just wasn't fair.

To the left of the sidewalk ran a large parking lot, along with the entrance to the Japanese garden.

Christine had never figured out how to craft a portal on her own, like Nikolai or Ty could. Without her earth power to ground her, she was certain she'd never be able to figure it out.

But even without her other powers, she'd always been able to activate existing portals and get them to take her where she wanted to go. Seattle had portals in every park she'd been in. The Japanese gardens should have a portal as well.

Fortunately, just two blocks away from her parents' house, on one of the docks, stood another portal.

While Christine could, technically, land just outside her parents' door, she never did. She didn't want to draw that much attention to them.

Plus, with her powers so out of control, she wanted a fixed location to aim for. She had to hold a very specific place in mind when she stepped into a portal, or it wouldn't work.

Christine nearly balked when she saw the entrance fee to the gardens. They wanted how much? She knew the gardens weren't that big or extensive.

She rationalized that it would still be cheaper than a taxi ride. And faster.

Christine stopped at the entrance of the park and studied the map. Hopefully there would be a clue there where the portal might be and she wouldn't have to wander aimlessly looking for a sheen of magic.

Ah. That had to be it. A *tori* gate, hidden in one of the far corners. The location on the map had that familiar gleam to it of someplace other, slick with rain that hadn't fallen in weeks.

The white rocks crunched under Christine's sandals as she hurried along the path. Graceful Japanese maples lined the way, their clumps of leaves artfully maintained, like clouds of Heaven. The big *koi* fish in the pond blurped at her as she crossed the bridge.

Were they warning her? Or just hungry?

No one else walked on the path as Christine slipped under the trees, heading for the gate. The air felt still there, as if she'd already walked away from the world. She felt a pang of guilt that the gate she approached was listed as *kitamon*, the northern gate.

Her powers all had compass directions. And she'd destroyed the things holding them, one by one. Desecrated the sites.

Christine shook her head. She couldn't think about that now. She was going to visit her family. To lay out what had happened, was happening to her.

To try to justify her current actions to them.

Christine paused for a moment. She thought about the dock near her parents' house. The crooked wood of the pier, bleached and gray. The smell of the water. The sound of quiet waves. The warmth of the sun-baked planks.

At the last second, just as she was about to take the final step, she saw something out of the corner of her eye.

It was a tiny creature, no bigger than her palm, with glistening black wings and whirling yellow eyes. It had a lizard-like body, long and slim, with yellow and white scales, tapering off into a tail.

An imp? What was an imp doing here?

Patrick the ogre called them flying rats. Even Tina didn't have good things to say about them. Nikolai wouldn't serve them at the store unless they were supervised by a known customer.

Gleefully, the creature jumped. It landed on her shoulder, tiny pinpricks of its claws digging into her skin.

Christine was so surprised she continued her last step, walking across the threshold of the portal.

But she'd lost the firm hold in her mind on where she'd wanted to go. The other portal slid away from her.

So she landed someplace else.

Christine used both hands to sketch the outline of a doorway in the air yet again. She was so frustrated she could spit.

However, nothing appeared between her hands, no comforting blue swirls. No hint of magic. Still.

She was stuck in the pocket world the imp had taken her to. Trapped, actually, but she wasn't going to let herself consider that. Not yet.

Dark gray sky spread above her, unchanging, a twilight world. It wasn't full dark and it wasn't light. Just gloomy. It hurt her eyes. She felt herself straining to see more.

A semi-circle of bristling pines lined the southern edge of the meadow where Christine stood. Or rather, she'd thought they were pines, until she'd gotten closer. While they grew needles, and they gave off a sickly sweet smell that was kind of like pine, the needles themselves were gray and hard. More like thin filaments of stone.

Christine had hurried back to the center of the meadow when a wind had suddenly stirred the trees and some of the needles had fallen. They stung when they'd stuck her. The one that had actually pricked her skin had started wiggling, as if it were alive and trying to dive into her. She'd pulled it out quickly and stomped on it before it had penetrated more than a quarter inch.

Going up the slope, away from the trees, was more grass-covered hill, leading up to barren rocks. A mist hugged the stones. It made Christine uneasy as it swirled, folding in on itself.

She suspected it was aware, like the fog in that other world. If she went up toward it, tried to escape up that way, the fog would attack her, she was certain of it.

The grass under her feet was a dark green and felt springy. It, at least, appeared to be just what it was, though Christine had only looked closely at it once.

She *had* to get out of here. She had no idea how long she'd spent in this place. It felt like hours, but had it been days? Or merely minutes?

The imp, of course, had just flitted away. It probably had its own way of getting between worlds.

Christine tried to form a portal again.

And failed. Again.

Colored lights that appeared to be hanging from a string circled her—jewel colors, green, blue, red, and white. Her air elemental had even helped her, setting them to float about five feet above the ground. They weren't any protection, Christine knew. They just made her feel better.

She hadn't tried practicing any other magic here. She felt less bloated, as if her powers had drained away slightly, leaving her merely satiated and not stuffed to the gills.

She'd abandoned the bag of tacos near the trees. They hadn't transitioned well to this world. The grease had congealed, grown hard as a rock. She would have broken a tooth trying to bite into one.

However, she was on her own here. She couldn't trust her powers not to try to burn down the place, or shake the trees and make them angry. Or attack the mist above her.

Though she suspected that if she was attacked here, her powers might suddenly start cooperating. At least until she was out of danger.

Suddenly, a blue swirling light appeared at the edge of the meadow, close to where Christine had first appeared.

Christine stayed where she was, drawing fire up into her hands automatically.

Yup, her powers would cooperate if there was danger. That was at least good to know.

Ty stepped through the portal. He had already half-transformed, looking as much wolf as man. His muscles bulged, and his hair stood all on end across his head and halfway down his neck, making him appear larger than he was.

"Oh, thank god," Christine said. She doused her fire and her lights and hurried over to where Ty waited.

The demon hunter peered at her intently. "You okay?"

"An imp attached itself to me when I was stepping through a portal," Christine told him hurriedly. "Dragged me here."

"Where?" Ty asked. "Where did it touch you?"

"Here," Christine said, turning and patting the back of her shoulder. *Ow.* That hurt. Why did it hurt? Why hadn't it healed?

"Could you show me?" Ty asked, stepping closer.

He was acting so stiff and strange. Why? It wasn't as if

she expected him to hug her—she didn't like touching anyone.

Christine was glad she was facing away as she tugged at her blouse, baring her shoulder to him. She couldn't see the marks, but now that she was thinking about it, they did sting.

She heard Ty sniffing the wounds. "Poison," he announced.

Christine shivered. What the hell? Imps were generally not poisonous.

"Come on. Let's get you home," Ty said. "We'll deal with the poison later."

Christine pulled her blouse back over her shoulder. "How did you find me?"

Ty shrugged. "Finding—hunting—that's what I do."

"But *why* did you come after me?" Christine persisted. She hadn't been expecting him, though he had promised to call her later that evening. After he'd finished running from whatever had been chasing him.

"Your brother called," Ty said. "Said you were late for dinner and he was worried about you."

Crap. She must be really late if he'd been that worried. Had she lost days?

Ty indicated that she should go through the portal first.

Christine gratefully stepped through…directly into her parents' living room.

Mum stood there with her arms folded across her chest, scowling.

Christine almost turned right around and stepped back through.

What had she done wrong now?

~

Though it was after ten PM, Mum and Dad still wanted the entire story, from the start. They all sat around the kitchen table, with Ty there as well. Christine didn't mind how closed in the room felt—she had too many good memories of meals with her family there. Plus, the white cabinets and yellow walls made the room seem cheery, particularly after being on that gray world. A bright warm spot, with the rest of the house dark, night settling in.

Christine told them about the broken buses, then the imp. Mum drank tea, of course, while Dad, Dennis, and Ty all had beers.

Christine hadn't wanted anything stronger than water. Now that she was back on the human plane, she felt overly full again. Stuffed. Unbalanced.

"The imp clawed my shoulder," Christine said. She reached up to pat the mark. Why didn't it hurt anymore? "But I'm better now," she said lamely. "You said the spot was poisoned," she accused Ty. Not a bad poison, or he would have done something about it in the pocket world.

He nodded. "It was. The place where the imp took you inhibited your ability to regenerate."

"Oh," Christine said. She healed fast as a troll—much faster than a human. She'd learned that after battling the demons six months before. Despite deep gouges in her arms, she'd still completely healed in about a week.

"I think that imp was following you from the time you

left your office," Ty said. "Did you have problems at the taco stand?"

Christine thought back and nodded. "Yeah. The register wouldn't take my card. So I paid cash." She paused, then added, "Did Lars set that thing on me?" She wouldn't put it past him.

Ty shrugged. "Don't know. It's possible. It may have also just decided to pick on you."

Christine bristled. How dare that thing? "Imps aren't generally poisonous, are they?" she asked.

"Not generally, no. This one was particularly strong. And nasty," Ty confirmed.

Christine nodded. Probably Lars, then.

"You *are* vulnerable right now," Ty said gently. "Until you get a better handle on the powers that you have, as well as regain your earth power, imps and other creatures are likely to pick on you."

Christine didn't like the sound of that at all.

"So what happened next?" Mum asked. "Did this… imp…kidnap you?"

"Kind of," Christine said. "I was going to use a portal to get here, after the second bus broke down."

"You should have called," Dennis said. "I would have come to get you."

"I wanted to solve the problem on my own!" Christine complained. She sighed in frustration when she realized how petulant she sounded.

"You don't have to, you know," Dad said gently. "We're here to help, too."

Christine nodded, feeling miserable. "I know," she

said. "But it's magic. And it's dangerous. And I don't want any of you to get hurt."

Mum seemed mollified at that. "So this imp took you to another world and you couldn't get back."

"I can't make a portal on my own," Christine told her. "Not until I get all my powers back. As Ty said, I'll be vulnerable until then."

"Dennis told us about your powers," Dad said. "How they're all elementals. And are bound."

"And that's the problem," Christine said. "This demon that bound my powers—Ming the Merciless—"

"Just Ming," Ty corrected. "Ming Dao." At Christine's gesture of invitation, he continued. "Ming works for the court. When a being has been found guilty of a specific type of crime, Ming will bind their powers. Make it so they can't commit the crime again, or harm anyone."

"Lars said that if I break the last of my bindings, all of Ming's bindings will be called into question," Christine said.

Ty nodded. "He's right. And they should be."

"What?" Christine asked. She hadn't thought that would be Ty's opinion. He was the one who found demons, brought them to justice, made sure they got bound in the first place.

"As you've said before, you aren't a criminal. Your powers shouldn't have been bound. That's illegal," Ty said. "It means that Ming has already been compromised. Who knows how many others are illegally bound?"

"So they'll examine all of his bindings?" Dad asked. "Not just the court-ordered ones?"

Ty nodded. "They'll do…magic, of a sort. To find them all."

From Ty's expression, Christine guessed that the magic Ming would be subject to wouldn't be pleasant.

"But some of the criminals who are legally bound will now get away," Dennis pointed out. "Like Lars. He said they'll find someone more amenable to bind him, this time."

Ty sighed. "That's always the possibility. Since Lars has bragged about it to witnesses, I can petition the court to look at his case separately."

Christine shook her head. "Lars is sneakier than that. He knows that's what you'll do. He'll already have contingency plans. He'll still get away."

"That may be the case," Ty said. "But once you find your earth power, you won't be as vulnerable when he comes after you."

"I still have a hard time believing the Sorgenfreys are demons," Mum said dismissively. "I just had tea with Mrs. Sorgenfrey this week."

"What?" Christine asked at the same time as Ty asked, "Where?"

Mum looked confused.

"You know she's in prison, right?" Christine said. "She and her husband and Lars kidnapped Tina?"

"That's right," Mum said slowly, nodding. "How could I forget that?"

"Magic," Ty replied dryly. "Where did you meet?"

"She sent me an email. No, a text message," Mum said. Her voice gained anger. "We met at the coffee shop just down the street. I swear it was her."

"It was just a visitation of her, a projection. She wasn't really there," Christine told her mum.

"I did wonder why she didn't have anything to drink," Mum said. "And she was trying to confuse my perceptions, wasn't she?"

Mum pushed herself out of her chair and marched angrily out of the kitchen, across the living room and looked out of the window, over the deck.

Christine and Dennis exchanged looks. Mum literally shook with anger. Had Christine ever seen her mum so pissed off? Possibly not.

Dad hastily scooted out of his chair and went to stand beside Mum.

"Just wait," Christine told Ty quietly.

Christine knew how angry she had been—though if she was honest, still was—when she'd learned about the changeling spell. How her very nature had been perverted. How she'd been given preferences and tastes that weren't really hers, but merely a mirror of Tina's.

How she still was learning her troll nature, always unsure what was really *her*.

She imagined her mum was feeling about the same. Pissed off that her perceptions had been altered. What had Mrs. Sorgenfrey said?

At least the demon hadn't been able to come into the house. Christine had spent a lot of money making sure that her parents' house had magical protection. *Ba gua* mirrors hung over the doors leading outside. Charms in tiny velvet pouches hid in the corners.

It wouldn't be enough. Not if a dozen or so demons made a concentrated attack. However, it would hold off the odd visitation, prevent two or three from just casually entering.

Dad put his arm over Mum's shoulder eventually. Was she crying? Christine's stomach fell. A minute later, they turned back, holding hands.

That was something Christine had learned to accept about her parents, that they held hands in public, even after all these years. As a teenager, she'd been embarrassed about it. Now, she thought it was kind of cool.

Mum sat down at the kitchen table, composed. Her blue eyes were like steel, and her face held great determination. She put her hands on the table and laced her fingers together. "First of all, I must apologize to you, Christine," Mum said. Her British accent was strong—another indication of just how angry she was.

"No, Mum—" Christine started.

"Let me finish," Mum said determinedly. "Mrs. Sorgenfrey played on my fears. That you were turning into some sort of creature. That I didn't really know you, that I never would know you." Mum took a deep breath. "I shouldn't have listened to her. I should have listened to my heart."

"Mum…she's a demon. Of course she's going to strike where you're most vulnerable," Christine said. She glanced over at Dennis. "You, too. And it wasn't just their words. They used magic, too, to influence you. Don't beat yourself up too much."

"You might want to think about personal protection charms for everyone," Ty suggested.

Christine sighed and nodded. She'd originally

considered getting some of those, but they were so expensive. Thousands of dollars each.

If only she could make her own…but she needed all her powers for that type of work. Plus training, she was certain.

Which Nikolai would be happy to give her. Along with all the ingredients. For a price.

"These attacks will just get stronger if you get your powers, won't they?" Dad asked. "Because the Sorgenfreys will no longer be bound at all."

Christine nodded. "Yes. But I may be able to protect you on my own, at that point." She didn't know what she'd be able to do as a magical troll. Nikolai had met only a few over the centuries, but even he didn't know the full extent of their powers. There were myths, rumors, legends, however, trolls tended to keep to themselves.

"I don't want that woman freed," Mum said sternly. "The kind of damage she'll be able to cause…" Mum shivered. Then she unlaced her fingers and put her hands flat on the table. "But I also don't want to see you sick like this."

"Like what?" Christine asked. She didn't think anything of her condition would show up in her human form. It was just an illusion, after all.

Mum considered her for a moment. "Puffy," she said. "Fevered. There's something wrong with your eyes. Dazed perhaps. They're not clear. You're not well."

Christine was impressed. Then again, this was her mother, who always knew that she was faking when she said she was sick just because she didn't want to go to school.

And who sometimes let her stay home anyway.

Dad clapped his hands, then rubbed them together. "All right, then. You know the consequences of your actions. We, as a family, agree with your choice, regardless."

Christine wanted to protest his choice of words. He made it sound as though they'd all agreed to be punished for the consequences of her choice.

Dad continued. "How can we help?"

"You can't," Christine said plainly. "It's too dangerous." Her fire elemental had badly burned Joe—she didn't know if it would have killed a human. Her air elemental had been too focused on her to kill anyone else, but if someone had been close, she wouldn't have put it past it.

Her earth elemental was likely to be the strongest of all her elements. She assumed it would be angry. Furious. And even more deadly.

Dad looked disappointed. So did Mum, actually.

Dennis just looked stubborn. He was likely to show up at her apartment without her inviting him over, she knew. "Just happened to be in the neighborhood" type of thing.

"Keep yourselves safe," Christine told them. "Check in with each other, every day. Make sure that you aren't being influenced. Dad, you weren't affected, right?"

Dad shook his head. "Don't think so." He shrugged. "Probably not important enough."

"No, that's not it at all," Christine assured him. "They'll probably reach out to you next."

Dad looked worried.

"I'll keep him in line," Mum said firmly.

"That you do, dear," Dad said, reaching over and squeezing her hand.

"So now, I just have to find my earth elemental," Christine said. "And hope the damage isn't too great when I free it."

She would survive one last battle. She had to.

Her family was depending on her.

CHAPTER 9

Dennis had wanted to bring up a map of Capitol Hill, plot out potential sites of where Christine's earth elemental might be, but she complained about being too tired.

She couldn't talk him out of giving her a ride home, and didn't really want to, anyway.

"Could I get you to promise me not to go looking for your earth elemental until Saturday?" Dennis asked as he drove up the hill. He blasted cool air from the vents in the dashboard. It had almost cooled off enough outside to be pleasant. Traffic had died and only a couple other cars were on the long stretch of road.

"Did you not hear what I said earlier?" Christine asked. "That it's dangerous? And no, you were not 'born ready'. You weren't born to handle this kind of thing. You're *human*."

Dennis shrugged. "You still need some kind of backup," he insisted. "And I take it that Joe isn't going to be your Prince Charming."

"He really isn't," Christine said. "I mean, it was nice, having another troll around. But he's not right."

"Not Mr. Right?" Dennis teased. "Just Mr. Right Now?"

Christine rolled her eyes. "Not even that," she told him. Though she'd miss Joe, if she was honest, she missed the potential of what they could have become more. Not what they'd had.

"So can you at least call Ty before you go get your next elemental?" Dennis asked, not letting go of the topic as they slowed down for the next traffic light.

"No," Christine told him. "He'd just get his ass handed to him as well." She paused, then let the illusion slip from her left hand and arm and held it out toward Dennis. "Have you ever felt troll hide?"

Dennis glanced over at her, then reached out and ran his hand along her arm.

"Can you feel how thick and tough that is?" Christine asked. "There's not much that will get through it. Ty has claws and fangs, but merely fur. He's not as tough as I am."

"Okay, so you're tough," Dennis said. The light turned green and he started forward again. "I get that. But you're still vulnerable, too. Who's going to watch your back?"

Christine thought about that for a long while after Dennis dropped her off.

In the end, she decided that there might only be one person strong enough to match her.

She put in a call to Tina.

～

"I'm so glad you called!" Tina said as Christine opened the door Saturday morning to let her in. "I've been thinking about you a lot."

It was always so weird for Christine to see Tina. They looked identical, yet opposite. While Christine was olive-skinned, with blue eyes and dark hair, Tina had the same peaches-and-cream complexion as the rest of the Tuckermans. She wore her blonde hair in a short page-boy that perfectly curled at her shoulders, a look that Christine could never have managed with her thick, uncooperative hair.

Since Christine's human appearance was now an illusion, she'd made some subtle changes to her own look, so they weren't so alike. She'd added mass to her body—broader shoulders, a larger chest, bigger hips. While she was aware that some people would think she was overweight, she knew that was just them. She didn't present as fleshy, but as muscled.

There wouldn't be as many men who found her attractive. But her appearance now better matched her sense of her own self: solid and strong.

Tina threw an arm over Christine's shoulder, giving her a brief hug. Christine allowed it, though it still freaked her out when her doppelganger touched her.

A part of her always expected the spell to be reversed, or something else to go awry when they touched.

Then Tina stepped back and looked at Christine critically.

Christine closed the door and shook off her illusion, letting Tina look.

"Wow," Tina said. "I would have said you'd been working out, but that isn't it, is it?"

Christine shook her head. "Turns out I have magical powers," she said.

Tina's eyes grew big. "Really? That's so cool!" Then she paused. "You know that generally, the only magical trolls are royalty, right?"

Christine nodded. Patrick had told her that long ago.

Plus, she still had that weird memory of her air elemental showing her the weeping troll king, sitting on his throne all alone, all his heirs gone.

Christine led Tina to the kitchen and made them tea while she told the story of Lars, finding the elements of her powers and breaking the bindings.

"That was you?" Tina asked, surprised. "I remember Mr. Slotski—my animations teacher—mentioning that earlier this week. How there was some kind of magical reckoning taking place in the city."

Christine nodded. "I just have one left. My earth elemental. It's likely to be the strongest."

"You want me to help you find it?" Tina asked. "Cool! Where do we start?"

"I plotted it out on a map," Christine said, leading them to the living room. Tina negotiated her way through Christine's piles of books as if she lived there. At least that hadn't changed—they were both still comfortable in this type of space.

Christine sat down next to Tina and showed her the map on her laptop. "Here are the places where I found the other elementals," she said. The points didn't map exactly to a compass. North-south was skewed. The eastern point wasn't directly in the middle, but more north. "I figure the western point must be down here," Christine told her.

It made sense, once Christine had remembered the sigil she'd seen at every location, the treble clef. The line across the center of that had been skewed as well.

"Awesome!" Tina said. "I'd be happy to help!"

Christine smiled. Though Nikolai had told her—often—that she couldn't trust a human, she did trust Tina. Tina had been pissed about not being able to find Christine's bio-parents, that the records were sealed. She'd also continued to defy her parents and go out with Christine several times a month.

Christine didn't trust Tina's parents as far as she could throw them. Did they know about her powers being bound? Had they been the ones responsible? She didn't know, but she wouldn't have put it past them.

Though they had the paperwork that showed they'd officially adopted Christine, they hadn't, really. They'd just used her, dropping her off with the Tuckermans while taking Tina from them. Possibly they felt it was the right thing to do, based on the oracles that had declared Tina's Destiny, but there was still something morally lacking in their decision.

Since the changeling spell had broken, the oracles now proclaimed that Tina's Destiny was hazy. They didn't say she didn't have one, but they weren't sure what it involved.

Was Tina's Destiny intertwined with Christine? Or did Christine have her own Destiny?

The pair of them drank their tea and talked of everything else—of Joe and how he wasn't Mr. Right, of Tina's own trials trying to find the right person (Christine being the only one who knew that Tina was as interested in women as she was in men), of learning magic and spells, of work and sundry.

Christine had found it easier to talk with Tina than most anyone. Then again, at one point, they'd kind of shared a body, all of Tina's tastes being reflected in Christine. That had changed slowly, but they still had enough common ground and experiences.

Plus, they shared tastes in books, and it was marvelous to be able to talk about favorite authors and recent reads with someone.

When they finished their tea, they went out and into the neighborhood. The day was overcast and muggy. Though rain was promised, Christine didn't believe the forecasters. They were probably lying. It wouldn't rain for months and months, given the moodiness of the clouds.

They walked up the hill, then left to begin their search. They went block by block, past grand old brick apartment buildings, Craftsman houses that had been subdivided and needed love, a BBQ in the park with a rollicking game of Frisbee played by three guys and a collie.

Christine was just about to suggest they walk up to the little Thai place and get something cool to drink when Tina stopped suddenly. "This way," she said, lightly running up a set of stairs.

Laurel trees stood at the top of a small hill, trimmed into a solid three-foot-wide hedge, maybe twelve feet tall. The sidewalk was stained with their fruit. Birds chirped, hidden in the waxy leaves.

Wasn't this a private residence? Next to the private school? It had that feel.

Christine shrugged and followed.

Ruins stood behind the hedge. Christine blinked, astonished. She'd never even suspected this was back here.

The first piece looked like the front of a temple. Which made sense, given that the school next door, as well as half of the rest of the block, was taken up with a modern Jewish synagogue. It was a single wall, with three arched doorways. Lighter, yellowish stone and brick made up the wall, forming geometric patterns.

Beyond the wall stood four tall pillars, each fifteen feet high. They were fluted, made from weathered stone.

Christine gaped as she walked between them, her eyes drawn inevitably up.

The tops of the pillars. Someplace high. Unable to touch the ground. Trapped in the air.

Old. Valuable. Historic.

This was where her earth power had been bound.

"Damn it," Christine said. She did *not* want to destroy this historic landmark. Though she couldn't sense her earth power here, she felt the history of this place.

It had been an important building, once.

She looked around. Hedges hid the ruin from the sidewalk. She could barely see the tops of the cars passing on the street. She never would have found this place on her own. She still had the feeling that this was private property. That she didn't belong here.

Maybe that was part of the magic protecting this place, making sure she didn't find it. "What did you sense?" Christine asked Tina.

Tina shrugged. "While it was kind of magic," she said

slowly as she walked around one of the center pillars, "it was also, well, kind of *you*."

Christine nodded. That made sense. Ty had said something similar. He'd caught a trace of her scent there.

"When I free my power," Christine told Tina, "I might end up breaking these pillars. And the gates. I don't want to do that."

Tina nodded. "Do you want me to try to hold the stones together?" she asked. "Or research how to rebuild it, afterward?"

"Both?" Christine asked. She wasn't sure what would happen. If Tina could possibly keep the pillar intact. Or if the entire place would have to be reconstructed.

They couldn't try to get Christine's power now. They would have to come back later that night, when there were fewer people around. Though no one could see them, it still made Christine uneasy to try to do magic in the middle of the bright afternoon.

The birds in the bushes and trees surrounding them suddenly startled, flying out into the open space. They formed a circle, whirling above Christine's head for a minute. Like a crown.

Then they dove back for cover.

Had that been a welcome for Christine? Or a warning? Or both?

Tina knocked on the door to Christine's apartment just before midnight. Christine was surprised both by how Tina was dressed, and by her thunderous scowl.

She wore a great black robe that hung down to her ankles, made of black satin embroidered with black thread that shimmered when Tina moved. Her wand was already in her hand—what looked like a human magician's wand, black plastic with a white tip. She wore a blood-red turban with a sparkling blue gem in the center.

She looked as if she was going to a costume party, dressed up as something like a magician or a witch.

Except that she also *glowed*, that blue tinge that spoke of her power, with her blonde hair spread out wide, as if she'd just rubbed her head with a blanket.

"I didn't tell my parents where I was going," Tina said. "But they knew. I know that news of your breaking your bindings—or at least, of something breaking free—has been everywhere. But they knew, they *knew*, it was you."

"Okay," Christine said, not really surprised that the Zimmermans had had a hand in her powers being bound.

"They told me that helping you was illegal, and that it would put the entire world in jeopardy," Tina fumed. "When I pointed out that you weren't a criminal, that your powers shouldn't have been bound in the first place, they hemmed and hawed, and mentioned something about the crimes of the father."

"Wait. So my powers were bound because of something my bio-dad did? That's just messed up," Christine said. Why would the Host and the court do something like that?

"That's what I said. They still told me I couldn't go out, *forbade* me," Tina said, still angry.

"So you snuck out?" Christine asked.

Tina gave her a huge grin. "Hell no. I *stormed* out.

Threw it in their faces that they weren't really my parents." She glanced down at her outfit. "They put me in these clothes, as if that was somehow supposed to stop me."

"Are they tracking you with it?" Christine asked. She wouldn't have put it past them to put some kind of watching spell on the cloth.

Tina shrugged. "Maybe. They don't really need to, do they? Not if they already knew about your powers being bound. They already know where we're going."

Christine sighed. She hoped she'd only have to battle with her earth elemental. That the Zimmermans didn't show up as well. "Will they get there before us?" Christine asked as Tina formed a portal with impatient gestures.

Tina paused for a moment. "I don't know and I don't care. I'd be happy to fight them if it came down to that. While they keep saying what they did to you was for the greater good, it still wasn't right."

Christine nodded, not surprised. She didn't know what she'd do if she found out her parents, the ones who had raised her, had done something as underhanded as the Zimmermans.

Then Tina shrugged. "Though, knowing them, they wouldn't come and fight themselves. They'd call someone else to do their dirty work."

"Might not be some*one* they call," Christine told Tina as she took her outstretched hand. "But a some*thing*. Since, as you said, it's obvious what I've been doing." Who knew what kind of favors were owed the Zimmermans, who were some of the most powerful magicians in the city?

"We'll be able to take whoever or whatever shows up," Tina said confidently.

Christine nodded as the magic closed around her, that sudden bump that told her she'd shifted places again.

Tina would try to help, Christine knew.

However, she also knew better than to rely one hundred percent on her human doppelganger.

Tina was human. Strong, powerful, but only human.

In the end, Christine knew she'd only be able to count on herself.

Christine and Tina stepped out of the portal onto the grassy area behind the hedges, well hidden from the street.

The four pillars shone softly in the muggy night, as if they'd been misted with dew. Just beyond them rose the large front of the temple, the three arches dark with mystery.

Between Christine and the pillars stood a tall Asian man. Though the top of his head was completely bald, he had a long, drooping black mustache. He wore a black silk robe that went down to his wrists and ankles, with a high collar as well. Christine would bet that in better light, she'd be able to see embroidery on it, also done in black silk. Probably dragons.

This had to be Ming Dao.

Christine understood the joke, now. Though Ming's face was round and his nose squished in, because of his long mustache, he bore a superficial resemblance to that movie character.

Ming stepped forward. "I cannot let you do this," he said. "You cannot unbind the last of your powers." He turned his glare to Tina. "And you should be home. In bed."

"You bound them illegally," Christine told him. "They're mine to take back."

Tina added defiantly, "I'm here to help my sister."

Ming bit his lips together, considering, before the words exploded from him. "You don't understand what you're doing! Neither of you! The consequences go far beyond you and your powers."

"I know that the rest of your bindings will be reexamined by the court," Christine told him. "How many other illegal works will they find? How long will your ass burn in jail?"

"You're missing the point," Ming said sternly. "Everything I've done has been to *stop* the Great War. All those who have been bound will be great fighters, later."

"You're a demon," Tina said. "You're born with a forked tongue. Why should we believe you? Your kind are the ones *starting* the Great War. You plan on winning it."

Christine looked more closely at Ming. She didn't see him as a demon. Her power stirred, considering, but she couldn't see through his illusion. He still looked human to her. Powerful, yes. Now that she concentrated on him, she could see the magic puffing him up, making him seem bigger and more important than he was.

But it bothered her that she couldn't see his demon

form. Even when her other powers weren't cooperating she could generally see through illusions.

Ming shook his head. "No," he said. "There are some of us who don't agree. Endless war—which is really the aim of the Great War—won't be good for anyone. Not even demons."

"Why are you telling *us* this?" Christine asked. "I would think you'd want to keep this a great secret. Hidden, you'd be able to do more."

Ming paused and studied Christine. "You're a clever troll, aren't you? I can see why they thought you a threat."

"Who are *they*? And why would I want an endless war?" Christine said, bewildered. "I don't want to put my family in danger."

Ming continued peering at her for a long moment before he shook his head. "Who knows what secrets trolls really hold in their hearts? Your kind is notoriously untrustworthy."

Christine stiffened. "Is that what you tell yourself? That we *deserve* it? So that you don't have to feel bad or even think twice when you steal another troll baby to be used as a changeling?" She'd never understood why so many trolls were taken as changelings. It had never made sense to her.

Were the trolls in Trollville so desperately poor that they had to sell their children into slavery? Or was there something else going on?

Christine stomped her foot, her powers swirling up inside her. "My people were not created to *serve* your kind," she said.

An ominous rumble followed her words.

"I see," Ming said quietly. "Your Destiny isn't merely to fight in the Great War, is it? No, but to be a leader among your people. That makes you the most dangerous troll of all. A princess with a cause. And the power to do something about it."

Princess? Christine had wondered for some time if she was royalty. Particularly after her air elemental had shown her the troll king sitting all alone.

"Princess?" Tina scoffed. "She's just a troll. A changeling to fool *your* kind, to preserve *my* Destiny. I'm the one you should worry about. Not her."

Christine blinked in surprise. The words stung.

Then she realized what Tina was doing—she was trying to draw Ming's attention to her, to leave Christine free to act.

"You're just a little girl in Daddy's robes," Ming threw back at her. "Untrained and unworthy."

"Untrained, huh?" Tina said. "Watch this." She pushed back her sleeve and readied her wand.

"No, don't," Christine said. She touched Tina's wrist. "We can't attack first," she said.

Tina looked at her quizzically. "Why not?"

Christine opened her mouth then shut it again. She didn't know why not. But she just knew that they couldn't.

Ming *had* to throw the first punch.

"She's right," Ming said. "But no one ever taught you that, did they?" His eyes suddenly flared red and bored into her. "Trolls are never the first to a fight. Not unless greatly provoked. For all their violent tendencies, trolls have more self-control than all the other *kith and kin*."

Christine hadn't known that. Ming had been right. No

one had taught her. It just felt wrong to start the fight. "I want my power, my earth elemental," she told Ming. "I am going to start calling it. Your choice is to get out of the way or start fighting."

Ming shrugged. Suddenly, he appeared much bigger than he actually was. "Then we fight."

Christine had faced demons before. It hadn't been fun. She'd been badly mauled, her left shoulder ripped to shreds, her stomach clawed, even her calves and feet suffered from bites and poisonous scratches. If she'd been a human, she would have died from her injuries.

However, that had been a purely physical fight.

Ming fought Christine and Tina with magic, sending a gout of flames at them. Huge sprays of fire sprang from his fingertips.

How the hell was Christine supposed to fight that? She couldn't punch the fire, let alone rip it to shreds with her own claws.

Fortunately, Tina had already set up a shield, protecting them. She sent a fire-hose-worth of flames back.

Christine found herself suddenly drenched in sweat from the heat. She was surprised the ground beneath them didn't just melt. The pillars behind Ming reflected the fire, their cool marble turning orange. Would anyone, any human, see the fire, and report it? She hoped not.

The two magicians threw more flames at each other. Christine felt useless. There wasn't anything she could do against such firepower. Her own flames would be just as likely to attack Tina as Ming.

Could she just physically attack Ming? He wouldn't be able to fight if he was flattened, right?

She raced toward him at full speed, arms out, ready to tackle him to the ground.

While Ming threw fire with one hand, he had some sort of shield that he maintained with his other hand. Christine smacked into it at full force, the blue flash momentarily blinding her as she landed on her butt.

Christine didn't have to see Ming's face to know he was laughing at her.

Fine. Christine didn't have her earth power. Not yet. She couldn't move the earth under his feet, not like she wanted to. Not like she *knew* she could, calling it to her, causing the ground to ripple like waves.

All she had were chunks of her power. Pieces of it. Illusions.

A big, strong demon like Ming expected to fight heavy-duty magic. Like what Tina had.

Maybe Christine could be sneaky instead. It wasn't a natural ability of trolls, she suspected.

But she didn't have to do what was expected of her.

While the battle raged beside her, the fires growing more intense, Christine called up her colored lights, two dozen of them, all hanging from an invisible string. They really were quite pretty, the reds and blues and greens warm in the night. Each light was about the size of her human hand.

It only took a little prodding—as well as pointing out the mischief these would cause—to get her air power to swirl the lights, first around Christine's head, then send them directly toward Ming.

The shield around him stopped them, of course. But the lights hung there, ominously twinkling.

Then they started pressing *in*.

Blue sparks flew, but the lights persisted.

Were they making headway?

Christine encouraged her air power to press a little harder while she readied her next attack.

Ming continued to focus on Tina, the heat from his latest attack billowing out over Christine. However, he took a step back from Tina and turned his body more towards Christine.

Christine couldn't see worry in his face. But she knew she had his attention.

Her little lights confused him. What could they be?

If only she had full control over her air elemental! She could start to suck the air out from his shield wall. Make it difficult for him to breathe.

That would be asking for too much from her air elemental, though.

The lights danced closer. Ming paused for a moment, gesturing with the hand he used to maintain his shield to push them away.

Christine felt the force behind his magic. If her little lights had been more solid, they might have blown up from the power. Instead, they bobbed a little, the bottoms of them drifting back, like lights hanging from a string and being blown in a strong wind.

But the string they were on held tight.

Ming returned another volley of fire with Tina then pushed again at Christine's lights.

This time, she was ready for him.

When he was focused on her lights, he wasn't focused on *her*. Or his shield.

With a mighty roar, Christine leaped into the fray, slamming her fist into Ming's shoulder, knocking him to the side.

Ming staggered back, but before he could raise his hand and blast Christine, Tina hit him from the side, spinning him around again. The tough hide on Christine's arm itched from the strength of the magical power.

But she wasn't burning.

Instead of casting huge gouts of flame, Tina had delicately coated Ming in ice.

Christine figured that the ice was to protect her, so she wouldn't be hurt. Her T-shirt was suddenly stiff and cracked loudly as she round-house punched Ming on his other shoulder.

The roar of the demon split the night. "I'm trying not to hurt you!" he yelled at them. "But you're making it awfully difficult!"

Christine roared her rage in return. How dare he treat her like some kind of…delicate princess?

Ming started to transform into his demon shape. Large, twisted wings sprouted from his shoulders. Hooks arched down from the tops of them. He had a serpent's head, with long fangs growing from his elongated face.

But before he could complete his transformation, Christine punched him again. And again. Stomping on his foot as it changed from human to hoof. Causing his long body to double over as it snaked along.

She pummeled that snout of his before he could start spitting venom at her.

Tina helped. She kept the demon encased in a golden light. Was it angelic? Christine didn't know. It sure did seem to slow Ming down.

Finally, Christine wrestled Ming to the ground. Tina cast golden ropes which wrapped around him firmly, so all he could do was squirm.

"Please, don't do this," Ming said, still trying to free himself.

Christine stared at him. "They call you *Ming the Merciless*. How many have begged you for the same?"

"They were different," Ming said haughtily. "I took those powers by order of the court. Which will be prosecuting you for this."

"Like how you took mine, at their order?" Christine asked, still angry.

Ming pressed his long mouth together.

"Who ordered my powers to be bound? Who are you working with?" Christine demanded.

Ming shook his head, refusing to say another word.

Christine turned to Tina. "Thank you," she said. "I'm not sure I could have done that without you."

"I still feel as though I owe you, for being stolen from your family, for all the things you've been through," Tina said quietly.

Christine opened her mouth, then shut it again. Tina wasn't the one who owed her anything.

But maybe, once Christine had all her powers back,

she could find those people. Those demons who had taken her.

Make them pay.

As Ming had said, as a troll, she would never strike first.

However, they'd already struck her, hurt her in the deepest places she had.

They'd taken away her earth power.

She'd get back at them. Each and every one of them.

CHAPTER 10

Christine tilted her head back and looked up at the top of the pillars. Her power was caged there, she knew. High in the air. Weakened, unable to mingle with its natural element, the earth.

Tina stood beside her, wrapped in her own magic, a golden light spilling from her. Ming lay bound behind them, arms tied down to his fingertips so he couldn't call up any more magic. Gagged so he couldn't do more damage with his forked tongue.

Christine told herself that he'd be safe there. Her earth power would have to go through her to get at him. She'd protect him.

The other powers inside of Christine lurched from side to side. She felt as though they were rolling their weight from one place to another, deliberately making her unbalanced. Though her air power had helped with the lights when she'd been fighting Ming, now it was done.

Were her other powers afraid of her earth power? It

was likely to be her strongest. Would it beat the others up? Make them fall into line?

God, she hoped so. She was so tired of their squabbling.

How was she going to free her earth power? It was bound differently than the others. Instead of being bound to one (or all) of the pillars, it felt caged, as though it existed behind cold prison bars. How did she break it out?

Christine didn't want to destroy the pillars if she didn't have to. They'd been part of the original temple that had once stood here. If they were desecrated, well, it was the demons who'd done that. Not her.

It didn't feel to Christine as if her earth power was aware that she was there. It felt as though it was asleep. She wasn't sure if that was a good thing or not. Maybe it wouldn't fight her as the others had.

How did she wake it up?

The answer was obvious, even to her smoke-clouded brain. Christine knelt slowly. The grass here had been watered regularly, so it was green and springy. She gathered up a patch of it, putting it to the side. Then she dug her claws deep into the rich earth and scooped out a handful before putting the patch of grass back on top of the hole she'd made.

Christine raised the earth to her snout and took a good, long sniff. It woke up her senses better than caffeine. The night was suddenly more light and alive, the air lay softer across her bare arms.

This. This would wake her earth elemental.

But how was she going to get up there? She didn't want to just fling the earth at the top of the column, hopefully getting some through the cage. Her own air elemental wasn't about to cooperate, either.

"Can I help?" Tina asked.

Christine nodded gratefully. There were some advantages to having a human doppelganger who was magically gifted.

Tina muttered a quick incantation. Suddenly, Christine started floating, heading up, straight for the sky.

She couldn't help but squirm. She wasn't afraid of heights, not really. But they made her distinctly uncomfortable. Particularly being up in the air like this, with nothing underneath her feet, nothing around her.

As Christine's head came level with the top of the center column, the night grew more dim and hazy. Was that the effect of the spell that was hiding her earth element? Or was it something Tina was doing, so no one could look up and see a troll floating so far above the ground?

If Christine had all her powers, she could probably make herself invisible. She was looking forward to experimenting with that.

Christine stopped going up when her waist was even with the top of the column. She looked around curiously. She could see less than she'd expected—only the street to the south. Buildings hid her view from the west and north, and tall trees grew to the east.

Though there was nothing on the top of any of the columns to prevent birds from nesting there, they were still remarkably clean.

The presence of her earth power probably kept them away.

Christine found she was still a couple feet away from the top of the pillar. She could just barely lean forward enough to grab the pillar and touch it. She bent her knees, bouncing a little, seeing how solid the magic was beneath her feet.

Heart pounding in her chest, Christine slowly slid one foot forward two inches.

The air under her held.

With great care, Christine shuffled forward until her toes touched the cool marble of the column.

Now what?

Christine looked at the earth in her palm. She brought it up to her nose for another good sniff of its wonderful bouquet. Then she pushed her hand forward.

"Wake," Christine commanded as she poured the dirt onto the top of the pillar.

For a moment, after Christine finished, nothing happened.

Then the tiny mound of earth started to glow. A golden cyclone spun the dirt around, turning all the grains brown, then blue. With a loud *whump* the cyclone flattened and blue light spread out to the tops of all four pillars. The treble-clef sigil sprang up on the top of each column, the light growing more and more intense. Arcs of lightning danced between the sigils, connecting them, sparking and hissing. The smell of the good earth tripled, as if Christine was suddenly buried. All her senses felt *alive*.

Christine squinted, trying to watch. Heat blossomed over her, as intense as when her fire elemental had first sprung up. Winds whipped around her, trying to flatten her. The air grew thick and muggy, making it difficult to breathe.

A booming *crack* filled the air. Christine threw her arm over her eyes for a moment.

When she lowered her arm, she saw another troll standing on the top of the pillar.

Her heart sank. She didn't recognize this troll. It didn't look like her at all.

First of all, it was a guy. He had long stringy hair that fell over one eye. The tusks rising up from his lower jaw were yellow with age, and one was cracked, the crown of it broken off. His green skin held gray scars, wounds improperly healed from some long-ago battle. He was still muscular and strong, despite how old he appeared. He wore a plain off-white tunic over cropped brown pants.

His bulbous nose kind of resembled the troll under the Aurora bridge, along with the long hair, but the resemblance was just superficial.

Was this her earth power? Christine reached out with her own magic, trying to find something of herself in this other troll.

There. Buried deep in his core was something that Christine recognized. Was that her? Or just some essence of troll that she felt kinship with?

"I thank you for waking me," the troll said. His voice was gruff, like boulders rubbing together.

"You're not what I was expecting," Christine admitted. How could she have been so wrong? Had Ming been wrong? He'd never actually said this was where her earth elemental was bound. Just that she couldn't do this.

Had he bound some other being there that he hadn't wanted her to find?

"Oh?" the troll asked. "What did you expect?"

It was funny, how still he seemed to be. Christine could sense the magic pouring out from him. He was probably the most magical being she'd ever met. Even more so than Tina, when she had her full magical glow on. But he was quiet inside. Not like Christine currently was, bubbling over with the water and fire elements, hissing at each other, her air elemental always whispering gossip that she couldn't quite catch.

"I'm looking for my earth elemental," Christine told him.

"I'm sorry," the old troll said. Then he peered at her. "You're a bit young to be a criminal, to have your powers bound."

Christine bristled. "I'm not a criminal," she said. "My magic was stolen from me."

The old troll shrugged. "Sorry. Can't help you there."

Christine peered at the other troll. Something was wrong with what he'd just said. He wasn't lying to her, not directly.

But he wasn't telling her the entire truth, either.

"Who are you? And why were you caged up here?" Christine asked.

"I, too, am not a criminal. Ming the Merciless caged me here. Unlawfully." The troll peered over her shoulder. "And I see you've brought him here for me, nicely tied up. I thank you for that."

"No," Christine said. "You can't just kill him. He needs to be brought to justice, before the Host."

The old troll gave her a gruff belly laugh. "Do you really think they'll punish him? No. They'll probably pat him on the back. Thank him for taking troublemakers like you out of their way. Do you really want that?"

Christine shook her head. "The Host will give him what he deserves," she said.

"Oh to be so young again. And so naïve," the troll said with great derision.

Christine rolled her eyes at that. Just because she was young (and possibly a bit idealistic) didn't mean she was stupid.

Besides, the longer she talked with the old troll, the more familiar he felt.

Was this actually her earth power, disguised?

He hadn't lied to her, or denied anything.

Then again, she hadn't asked him directly yet, either.

"Are you my earth power?" Christine asked, watching the old troll carefully.

"Why would think that?" he replied, scoffing.

Yes, there was something there. Some attraction.

"Are you my earth power?" Christine asked again.

"Do I look like you?" the old troll asked, his eyes narrowing, growing serious.

In the stories and the fairy tales, magic always happened in threes.

"Are you my earth power?" Christine asked a third time.

The old troll pressed his lips together, the muscles along his jaw clenching tightly. But he couldn't keep the words in.

"Yes, I am," he finally admitted. "Curse you! I was almost free."

With that, the old troll shrank in on himself. His skin grew lighter, his hair shorter. In just a few moments, Christine found herself facing, well, herself. Or at least a good semblance of what she regularly saw in her bathroom mirror when she was in her troll shape.

Were her shoulders really that broad? And her breasts that big? Huh.

But this troll's eyes were much harder than hers. And there were still scars on her arms, gray with age. What past trauma had caused those?

"Don't think you've won yet," the earth power said as it reached across the space between them and grabbed Christine's arm.

The other troll was stronger than Christine. She jerked Christine up and pulled them close together.

The smell of earth surrounded Christine. Not the good, fertile kind, but something wet and mucky that had been steeped in brackish water. The other troll wrapped her arms around Christine, pulling her closer to her chest.

Christine struggled to get away. She resisted hitting her earth power. She thrashed and pushed but it was useless.

The other troll felt *solid* in ways that Christine had only ever dreamed about. As strong as a mountain. Bones made of stone. A stillness ran through her earth power, deeper than the ocean.

The presence of the other troll surrounded Christine, wrapped itself all around her, trapping her, causing her to sink deep inside, until she was fully subsumed.

Crap.

Now what was she going to do?

She hadn't tamed and captured her earth elemental.

Instead, it had captured *her.*

~

Christine sank deep into the core of her earth power. It was like sliding into cool water on a hot and muggy day. It soothed her in ways she hadn't expected. She hadn't thought about her skin feeling hot or being irritated, but now, she realized that it hadn't ever been quite right.

Now she smelled the solid earth, clean and fertile, not the brackish spoiled part that she'd sensed when she'd first touched her earth power—that had just been the top layer of her earth power that had been corrupted. Christine tasted it too, warm and comforting, like her mum's homemade beef stew. Everything felt muted, all sound muffled, as if the traffic in the street was far away.

However, despite how wonderful it felt to revel in the power and solidness of her earth power, it was still a cage. She still needed to get out.

She was the one who needed to be in control, not her earth power.

Christine found that she could still see and hear, trapped all the way inside there. It was like watching a screen, though. She couldn't feel the heat of the night, the cool pillar under her feet.

The earth elemental looked down, over the edge of the pillar, toward the ground. A long ways down there stood

Tina. She still glowed with her magic. She mouthed the words, "You okay?"

The earth elemental waved cheerily, then gave a thumbs up.

Bitch was going to try to fool Tina.

Christine was torn between being furious that that her earth power was even going to try, and curious if Tina would be able to figure it out on her own.

When Tina raised her wand again, the earth elemental shook her head.

Christine felt the all-encompassing *joy* the earth elemental felt as it bent its knees, swung its arms back and forth a couple of times, then jumped.

The shock of being airborne held Christine completely still. What the hell was her earth power thinking? Hitting the ground was going to *hurt*.

Christine felt her earth elemental bracing for impact. *Wham.*

Her troll-self absorbed the impact as much as possible with her knees, then continued to bleed off the momentum by doing a summersault.

When it stood, it laughed, a great, happy laugh.

I'm free! came through loud and clear.

Christine couldn't help but grin. Her earth elemental's joy was contagious.

She also felt its relief. While it had been strong before, it grew even stronger now that it was touching the earth again. It sent power out, sinking it deep into the ground. Strength came pouring back, racing up from the earth, filling her bones. The stones below her sang with her earth elemental's joy.

A pale cloud appeared beside Tina. It quickly resolved into a being—Lars. He was still tall and pale. Had he lost weight while he'd been in jail? His T-shirt read "Chaotic Evil means never having to say you're sorry."

Tina didn't seem bothered by his presence at all. Why? Shouldn't she have flinched? Or punched him, or something? Why wasn't she reacting?

Lars leaned over and told Tina, "That's not Christine, you know."

Tina's eyes grew clouded. Even from a few feet away, Christine could see the haze gather, Tina's bright blue eyes turning gray.

How was Lars influencing her?

Oh, right. Demon.

The earth elemental didn't understand what was happening. It recognized Tina as a friend.

Did that mean that the doppelganger spell had been cast before Christine's powers had been bound? Or was the spell just that strong?

The earth elemental didn't know what Lars was. Lars wasn't really there. He was just a projection. So her earth power couldn't identify him as a demon.

Watch out! Christine tried to warn her earth elemental.

It didn't heed her, however. Instead it took another hesitant step toward Tina. This was her friend, right? Her human doppelganger?

Tina raised her wand slowly, her clouded eyes staring directly at Christine. "You're right. That's not Christine."

The blast of power knocked the earth elemental back on its ass. It roared its frustration.

It couldn't just sink into the earth. There was too

much concrete in the way, rubble from the building that used to be here.

Instead, it stomped the ground.

A loud rumbling followed.

Christine watched, fascinated, as the ground rippled out, as if her earth elemental had just dropped a large stone into a calm lake.

Tina was too focused on Christine to look around her.

Lars wore a satisfied, smug smile.

With horror, Christine realized what was happening.

Her earth elemental was about to cause an earthquake. And Lars would blame Christine. Declare it to the court under oath.

~

Christine cringed as Tina blasted her earth elemental again. That *hurt*. All its skin felt as though it was on fire. It was difficult to breathe, too, as if the blast had actually been a physical blow.

Let me help! Christine screamed, trying to get the attention of the creature binding her.

Her earth elemental ignored her. "Why are you doing this?" it asked. The voice sounded like Christine's. It also sounded as hurt and confused as Christine felt, that Tina, her human doppelganger, was attacking her.

Tina hesitated. Hope rose up through Christine. Would she stop?

However, Lars still stood beside Tina. Still influenced her. "Keep attacking," he commanded.

Tina obediently sent another magical blast at Christine.

Damn it! Was this why Nikolai had said to never trust a human? Because they were too easily influenced by demons? They didn't have enough will of their own?

At least Tina wasn't using all her power. Otherwise, Christine was pretty sure she'd be dead by now.

Tina kept blasting Christine, often enough that she couldn't think about rushing at the human.

The earth elemental gathered its own power. Its plan was clear to Christine—it was going to ripple the earth and topple Tina over. Dump her on her ass.

Let me help, Christine said again.

How?

Christine was surprised by the question. She wasn't exactly sure herself..

The fire elemental pressed up hard against Christine, trying to get her attention. It knew of a wall, a kind of a shield, that it could do. That would guard and protect them.

Christine was surprised that her fire elemental wanted to help.

Then again, if they didn't stop Tina, her earth elemental would end up killing them all.

"Here," Christine said, passing along the piece of information her fire elemental had handed to her.

The earth elemental gratefully put up the shield. The next blast from Tina didn't hurt nearly as badly. The earth elemental laughed. It shot power down through the earth, searching for pockets, for weak spots.

It was going to cause the earth to ripple. And not just here, no, the effect would run for miles.

Not only would Tina fall over. All the buildings nearby would too.

Christine had to stop it.

However, as the fire shield went into place, Christine felt the elements inside of her starting to integrate. It was like two puzzle pieces sliding together. Her earth elemental and her fire elemental were interacting. Working together.

Not only that, the integration point provided a chink in the cage that held Christine. It was an opening. A hole she could escape through.

It just needed to be a bit bigger.

Here, Christine said. She handed over a tiny bit of wind, that the earth elemental could use to push back at Tina.

With glee, the earth elemental shoved a wind at Tina's next blast, knocking it off track so it was merely a glancing blow.

The earth elemental laughed again. It was having too much fun, now, to want to end the game so soon. It blasted Tina again.

Christine shook her head. That wasn't good. If her doppelganger wanted to fool the human, it should continue to plead with Tina. Laughing just told the human that the troll she faced wasn't one she knew.

"Ice," Lars suggested to Tina.

Christine knew her fire shield wouldn't help. She didn't suggest anything, though. She let her earth elemental be blasted again.

More, the earth elemental demanded from Christine as it shivered and tried to breathe through the painful cold.

The cage containing Christine deep inside of her own power already had two chunks removed from it, from the two times her earth elemental had used the powers of her other elements.

Her powers had started to integrate. Soon, none of them would hold mastery over her, or the others.

If she got her air power and her earth power to work together, would that be enough for her to take control?

With hesitation, Christine offered up a bit of air from her water elemental, those bubbles that had helped her breathe when she'd been battling her air elemental.

The earth elemental took a great, deep breath of air. It shivered.

She'll stop attacking if you give me control, Christine pointed out. *It's hard being a troll.*

The earth elemental sighed and nodded. It wanted its freedom, so badly. But it also enjoyed the other powers, the warmth of the fire, the smugness of the air. It knew that it would be even stronger with all of them together.

The next blast from Tina sent shards of ice deep into the earth element's skin. It roared with pain and displeasure. It stomped the ground again, but it wasn't focused. The tremor it caused wasn't enough to do more than make Tina and the pillars beside them sway slightly, as if hit by a sudden gust of wind.

You can't win, Christine said. *She'll only stop once it's me again.*

Still naïve, the earth elemental replied. *She isn't really our friend.*

However, the earth elemental didn't like being in control as much as it had thought it would. It wasn't merely of the earth.

It was of *Christine*.

The other powers had reminded it what it of would be like to be whole.

The earth elemental started to relinquish control.

It sank, slowly, into Christine. It was the oddest feeling, as the power grew in the center of Christine's chest, then lowered, sliding down into her belly, as if she'd just become a mountain herself, solid and unmoving.

The winds around the mountain chilled and grew still, whispering their mischief and tugging at the grasses there. Water trickled down from hidden spring, laughing and teasing. The fire burned deep inside the mountain, threatening to erupt at any time.

Christine shook her head as she bobbed up consciousness.

She carried a multitude inside her, now. All her powers, safe. They weren't fully integrated, she knew that. It might take a lifetime of experimentation to get them to cooperate fully. There would always be times when they'd squabble.

However, they were all anchored to her earth power, now.

Christine couldn't wait to start her experiments.

But first, she had to stop Tina.

"It's me," Christine said as she stepped forward.

Tina blasted her again, this time using both fire and ice.

"Stop that!" Christine yelled.

She raised her arm and deflected the next blast from Tina. Christine's fire elemental surged up, the power bubbling over. However, she managed to send the blast from her own palm to the side so it didn't engulf Tina in blistering heat.

Not that Tina would have cared. Her eyes were still glazed over. She didn't have any will of her own.

Lars continued to stand next to her, smiling smugly.

Christine could see the illusion, now. Lars wasn't really there. It was just a projection. She was surprised that it was her air elemental that gave her the sight, that enabled her to see magic and pierce through illusions and projections.

Then again, her air elemental was the most informed of all her elements, the winds carrying tales from all over the world. It grudgingly shared the ability with Christine. She knew that there were many, many other things that her air elemental knew, that it might or might not ever tell her about.

She couldn't worry about that now. She had to stop Lars. Stop his influence over Tina.

But how?

When this battle was finished, Christine was going to have a long talk with Tina about better protection charms for herself and her family.

As Christine expected, when she sent a gout of flame at Lars, it passed directly through him, not hurting him in the least.

"Did you see that?" Christine asked Tina. "He isn't really here. He's just a projection. From *prison*."

Tina hesitated again.

"Not for long," Lars assured Christine. "Thanks to you, I'll be free soon."

"Tina, blast *him*, not me," Christine told the girl as she raised her wand. "He isn't your friend. He kidnapped you. Tried to twist your *Destiny*."

"That may be," Lars said with a shrug. "But *she* isn't your friend either," he added, indicating Christine. "She isn't the same troll that you floated up to the top of the pillars."

Christine was fascinated by how Lars was twisting the truth. He was absolutely correct. She wasn't the same troll. She had all her powers, now. And they were starting to integrate. She didn't feel so full and bloated. She felt solid. The night held secrets she longed to go explore.

As did the earth under her feet.

However, Christine didn't know enough. When she took another step toward Tina, she got blasted with a stupid lightning bolt. The energy dissipated around Christine's shield, shocking her badly.

How did she stop electricity from getting through?

She drew a blank. Neither her earth nor her air powers could help her.

Maybe there was a formal spell she could learn. *Deflect lightning bolt.*

If she survived this.

Her earth elemental suggested another earthquake.

However, Christine wasn't interested in leveling the city.

Instead, she directed her attention at the large rocks that lined the edges of the walkway, leading back from the center arch in the gate. They were each about knee high, maybe two feet across, artfully placed.

Christine touched one with her power. The stone was silent. It didn't sing or mourn as the stones on the bridge had.

It was dumb.

That didn't mean she couldn't use it.

Without much effort, Christine wrapped her power around the rock, then heaved it through the air.

Not at Tina, but at Lars.

Her aim was perfect, for once. The rock landed exactly where Lars was standing. He appeared to be cut off at the knees.

"Tina! Look! Please!" Christine shouted. "He isn't there."

The image looked like a bad Photoshop picture, with Lars not blended into the rest of the scenery, just stuck there.

Tina looked. She froze for a moment. Shook her head.

Her eyes cleared.

She glanced at Christine, then back at Lars. "Get the hell out of my head!" she yelled.

Instead of blasting him, which Christine had to admit she would have really appreciated, Tina did the next best thing. She directed her wand at herself. Glowing light sprang up all around Tina, a green globe, as she cast a protection spell..

Hopefully it was strong enough to ward off Lars and his influence.

"Christine?" Tina called, glancing at her, but then directing her focus back toward Lars.

"It's me," Christine said gratefully. "With all my powers." She couldn't describe how she felt. Strong, yes. At peace in a way she'd never imagined. Solid as the mountain, yet still as nimble as a spring breeze.

She felt good. Whole.

And wholly pissed off at Lars.

"I'm so sorry," Tina said. She stepped to the side, away from Lars, coming closer to Christine. "He just—he was in my head. Again. Evidently he'd left what I guess you'd call a backdoor into my psyche. That I hadn't found."

Christine nodded. That didn't surprise her.

There might be more traps that the demon had laid for her human doppelganger as well, that Tina would only discover at the right time. Or the exact wrong time.

Maybe Nikolai was right. Maybe Christine couldn't trust a human. Particularly one who had been captured by demons once.

Did that mean she couldn't trust her family anymore?

Christine couldn't think about that right now.

"So what do we do about him?" Christine asked, pointing to Lars.

"Do you have all of your powers?" Lars asked. He finally moved, stepping around the stone that Christine had lobbed at him.

Christine nodded, not trusting the demon.

Wait. Was he growing more solid? He looked less like a bad movie projection and more like a Hollywood version, one done with much better CGI.

"Good," Lars said, clapping his hands together.

The sound echoed in strange ways, like a far-off crack of heat lightning.

How could he make such a sound when he wasn't a physical being?

"Then it's my turn to fight," he announced.

A sudden blast of power scorched Christine's skin. She flinched and stepped back, averting her eyes.

Demons surrounded her. And Tina.

Scaly, nasty demons with great claws and teeth.

Demons ready to rip them both to shreds.

CHAPTER 11

"What the—" Christine began.

That was all she could get out before the first demon leaped at her, prepared to rend her to pieces. The color of dirty ice, it had a snakelike head and long, yellow fangs. Abortive wings fluttered on its shoulders, like an extra pair of hands, sickly white, tipped with claws.

"No!" Christine shouted as she punched it in the muzzle. Teeth broke against her knuckles, scraping her tough hide.

She was going to be so sore in the morning.

While her powers could have helped, she didn't have time to call on them, to learn their ways and tricks. She was too busy fighting a half-dozen assailants. They weren't that strong, but they were quick.

And there were many of them, constantly darting in to claw at her skin, bite at her unprotected back.

She tried to keep track of Lars while she fought. This wouldn't be his only ploy. Plus, if he'd wanted the demons to kill her, wouldn't he have conjured something bigger and deadlier?

Maybe he was trying to influence Tina again? Keep her distracted? She did have her own flock of demons to fight. She kept them at bay with firepower, or with ice. Her group was smaller than Christine's. But just as ugly, with mottled yellow and sickly green scales, lizard-like snouts and sharp teeth.

Lars stayed on the sidelines, grinning like a damned fool.

With horror, Christine realized that he was growing more and more real every minute.

He was manifesting, no longer content with merely projecting.

With an angry growl, Christine threw her arms around three of the demons at the same time, smashing them together then casting them to the ground, where she could stomp on them solidly.

As soon as she had a clear opening, she ran toward Lars.

He couldn't be allowed to come here. Not yet.

It wasn't that she was frightened of him. She *wanted* to fight him.

But not now. Not until she was fully integrated. Not until she had more of a clue about how to work with her powers.

She suspected that her powers would happily unite against Lars. They knew he was a demon, and probably indirectly responsible for binding them in the first place.

However, she didn't pause to try to blast him with ice, or fire, or anything like that.

She plowed directly into him, tackling him to the ground.

"Umph," Lars said, shaking his head.

He was corporeal. And just starting his transformation from human to demon.

"Oh no you don't," Christine told him. She smashed her fist into his face as hard as she could, crumpling the budding snout.

Lars screamed in pain.

Claws dug into Christine's shoulders. Sharp pain blossomed across her back.

Christine wouldn't let go. Wouldn't let herself be tossed to the side. Wouldn't let herself become just a *distraction*.

She reached up with one hand, beyond Lars' shoulder, up to his wings, tearing at the flesh between the bonelike struts with her own claws.

Lars heaved himself up, undulating his spine like a snake's, throwing Christine off her perch.

Huh. She didn't know he could do that. She scrambled to her feet, calling all her powers to her.

He rose up, growing quickly until he towered over her.

"Puny troll," Lars growled at her. "You may have been clever, getting your powers. But you're not strong enough to take me. I will take them, all of them, for myself now. Delicious powers."

Christine snorted. It wasn't that she thought she could win. She might not be able to.

But Lars needed to come up with better lines if he viewed himself as some sort of arch villain.

Letting a tiny, *very* focused fraction of her earth power

free, Christine stomped the ground, causing it to split under Lars' feet. Only a few inches, but enough to wipe the smugness from his face.

"Time to die," he announced.

Christine didn't believe in profanities. There had to be more clever insults that she could throw than "Go back to Hell.".

She'd have to think of some later. For now, all she could do was gather all her power together and withstand the first blow from Lars, his power already collected into a great ball that he was about to throw at her.

It was likely to be a doozy.

~

Lars threw yet another electric bolt, shocking Christine hard enough to make her stumble back. She shook her head, dazed, black spots dancing before her eyes. She smelled smoke, probably the sizzling of her own neurons. Possibly her hair as well.

Damn that hurt. She knew that becoming stone wouldn't help her. He'd just shatter her with the next blow.

She was really going to have to learn some sort of protection from lightning spell.

But maybe earth…When Lars hammered Christine again, she melted into the ground, becoming like a mound of dirt, absorbing the blow and dispersing it below her.

Lars snarled at her. "Too fast. You're learning too fast." He blasted her again before she could prepare, the power bowling her over.

As Christine scrambled to her feet, she looked past Lars to where Tina still fought her own demons. The human magician was trying to free herself, but every time she defeated a foe, another one sprang to life.

Christine narrowed her eyes, just for a moment.

Were Tina's opponents real? Did they actually physically manifest? Or were they as numerous as the human's fears and powers? The demons wavered momentarily.

Before Christine could call out a warning to Tina, she summersaulted, getting out of the way as Lars threw another bolt at her.

What did Christine have to attack him? She'd love to mash his face into the ground. To stomp his feet and break his toes. To tear—oh.

Christine's air power stirred, happy to be given a direction.

Lars had huge wings, that looked like they were made of black leather, the struts like white bone. Great hooks rose off the tops of the wings and hung over his shoulders.

Christine's air power sent great winds directly into his wings.

Throwing him off balance as the wings filled with air.

Lars waved his arms and cast some kind of spell to cut off Christine's winds.

However, while he was distracted, Christine lobbed another stone at him. This didn't hit him squarely as she'd intended, just giving him a glancing blow on his knee.

It angered him, though. He hadn't been expecting it, that was for sure.

Before Christine had the chance to celebrate her tiny victory, Lars snarled. "So you want to play with rocks?"

Suddenly, all the stones along the path rose up, two dozen or so.

Then headed directly for Christine like over-powered cannonballs.

~

Christine batted another stone out of the way, aiming to send it directly back at Lars but knowing she wouldn't succeed.

Damned demon was too slippery.

She was getting desperate. Her powers were exhausted. None of them were used to fighting like this. She didn't know how to just use a bit of each, and let it rest while she moved onto the next. She just kept calling one up after another. If only she had a bit of time—the earth might be able to renew her.

Lars wasn't giving her even a moment between attacks.

Tina was starting to diminish as well. Her bright magical glow was fading.

Christine needed to do something. Fast.

Her air power stirred, carrying the memory of the sigil Christine had found at each of the sites where her powers had been bound.

What was that symbol? Why was it familiar? Was there power in it, by itself?

Christine endured another blast of fire from Lars, throwing back her own ever-weakening flames. She'd tried stealing all his air, but he'd broken through her spell. She could, of course, cause a major earthquake, but she'd damage much of the city if she did that.

Plus, there was that sigil. Now her air power reminded her of how it had sunk into every stone of the bridge.

Why was that important? What did it matter if those stones knew her? All the stones here were dumb. Unaware.

Could she wake them up?

What would happen if she did?

Would they obey her? Do her bidding? Stop doing what Lars wanted them to do?

As Christine threw more power into her ever weakening shield against Lars' next flame attack, her water power surged up.

There wasn't any water nearby that she could direct… or was there? The grass under her feet, before it had been charred with magic, had been thick. Green. Well watered, during a season when there hadn't been any rain.

Which meant there was a sprinkler system. It didn't take too long, particularly with Christine's water and earth elements working together, for her to trace the path of the water lines underground.

Huh. There were water jets right under where Lars stood.

Instead of directing her next blast at Lars, Christine *pushed* her power under the ground.

An ominous rumble followed.

Suddenly, the sprinkler under Lars' feet erupted with water.

Then Christine's fire elemental quickly turned the water to flame.

The attack didn't come directly from Christine, so it was under and behind his shield.

Lars shrieked in pain as he redirected his own magic, trying to protect himself.

The sound filled Christine's heart with joy.

While he was distracted, Christine used her earth and air elements to set her sigil on the stones beside her, around her, behind her, in front of her. All the stones that Lars had been throwing at her. They lay like fallen soldiers on the battlefield.

They weren't alive like the stones of the bridge.

Christine was certain she could still make them sing.

The stones suddenly recognized her. Power arched from one to the next. Brilliant blue sizzling light sprang up. Even the stones that lay behind Lars lit up.

The crack that Christine had initially opened in the earth under Lars' feet suddenly filled with light as well.

There was something to that sigil. Something powerfully magic about it. Marking a stone or something with it bound that element to her.

She knew she couldn't use it on the grass or on a tree. Probably not even a body of water.

But the earth. And the stones. They were *hers*.

And they, too, had had enough of Lars.

"What are you doing?" Lars asked as he looked up. He sounded surprised.

Possibly worried.

"Binding you," Christine growled. She directed the stones to float closer to Lars. Not attack.

Lars sent his next blast of power at the stones, but they held firm and drew closer. Circling in.

They caged him in, encased him in the lines of glowing light emanating from every sigil etched into the side of each rock.

Christine couldn't really bind Lars' powers. Not like hers had been bound. She didn't know how. She was pretty sure she might be able to learn, though. Which was kind of a frightening thought.

She wasn't a demon. But she might have some demon abilities.

The brilliant blue lights drained Lars' power. Bled off the demonic energy. Charged the stones and the earth, making them stronger.

Lars kept blasting at the rocks. He tried fire, ice, even pure power.

The rocks didn't move away. They drew closer still.

Lars didn't have enough strength to power a mountain.

Christine did.

"You can't use the royal symbol that way," Lars told Christine. He sounded really worried.

Royal symbol? What did he mean by that?

Was that why Christine recognized the sigil? Because she was royalty?

"Yes, I can use it that way," Christine said, absolutely sure of herself. "You are a threat to the entire realm. Not just the human worlds."

As she spoke, she heard that bell-like ringing that she'd heard when she made a promise.

She'd just declared Lars an enemy. Possibly of all of Trollville. Probably of all trolls.

Christine wasn't certain of the consequences, but she

was pretty sure she'd be happy to pay whatever price was necessary at this point.

"You'll regret this," Lars said as he shrank back down to human form.

The rocks squeezed in closer still. He couldn't move a foot in any direction. Including up.

"I might," Christine said. "But you will cease this battle."

Lars stood up straighter, glaring at her. "I will. For now. But we will be joined in battle again. And soon." He threw his hands out in a wide gesture, barely avoiding smacking one of the glowing rocks hemming him in.

Then he stood there, blinking, surprised.

Obviously, he'd been expecting something to happen.

Nothing did. He still stood, enclosed in Christine's glowing lines of blue.

"Let me go," he ordered Christine.

"No," came an unexpected voice.

Ming Dao strode up to the center of the area.

How had he gotten loose from Tina's bindings? Was it because she'd been so distracted and had been attacked by Lars' demons?

"You will all attend the Host," he announced loudly. He clapped his hands together.

Christine's lights extinguished abruptly. The stones fell down to the earth, landing with solid *thumps*. The power they'd carried dissolved into the ground.

Suddenly, Christine felt a trickle of magic under her feet, tickling her soles. As she took a deep breath, it seeped into her. She was no longer as tired as she had been.

Was that how she was supposed to fight? Leave a part

of herself in the earth so it could keep coming back and refreshing her?

She was *really* going to have to experiment with that.

Tina lurched over to Christine. She was bleeding and pale, her gown shredded by demon claws. She had a huge gash under her chin, and the hand still clutching her wand shook.

"There were so many of them," Tina whispered.

"Were they real?" Christine asked quietly.

Tina blinked at her. "Oh no," she said, raising the hand without the wand up over her mouth. "Oh no!" With a grand wave of her wand, she disappeared.

"Why does she get to go?" Lars asked. He sounded like a teenaged boy asking why his sister got all the attention.

"She'll be there. At the court," Ming promised. "She has been served."

Ming turned to face Lars. "Christine hasn't bound your powers. But I will bind them again. I bear witness to your violating your parole by attacking the princess troll."

Princess troll? Christine shivered. Ming wasn't joking. Was she really royalty?

"She threw the first punch," Lars said nastily.

"No, she didn't," Ming said. "You caused the demons to attack her. That was the first blow."

Lars scowled. Obviously, he hadn't been expecting that.

"Papers have been served on all parties," Ming declared. "You will all have your day in court."

With that, Ming disappeared.

Lars snarled at Christine. Before he could say anything, though, a great swirling void swallowed him.

It looked as though he hadn't left on his own accord.

Thank you, Christine told her inner powers.

Whatever happened next, she knew she would at least have them to help her face it.

A golden light reached up from the ground, whirling around Christine. It reeked of paperwork and orderly procedures, bureaucracy and the law.

With a nod, Christine stepped into it.

And stepped directly into the hallway outside the court of the Host.

The hallway outside the courtroom was empty. Shouldn't there be guards outside? It was a Saturday night. Maybe the court didn't pay overtime. Beige tile covered the floor, and the walls were that government white, not quite dingy, but close. Dark wood made up the doors themselves, with old-fashioned scrollwork around the edges. No windows—Christine had the impression that this room was in the basement of whatever building contained it.

Christine looked down at herself, dismayed. She really didn't want to appear in front of a judge dressed as she was, in a torn and muddy black T-shirt, shorts spattered with mud, blood, and whatever ichor those demons had excreted, as well as bare feet, her claws broken and ragged.

Maybe she didn't have to go fully human, though, to change her appearance.

Christine put her hands out in front of her, willing them to at least *look* clean. (She was already anticipating the long, long, *long* soak in her tub with enough Epsom salts to turn the water blue.)

Her earth power helped. She wasn't sure why that elemental held the magic that let her disguise herself. Maybe it was because her earth power also held her true form, kept her toes rooted in the earth.

Her skin changed to a darker shade of green, the same shade she'd originally seen her earth power wearing, not the usual brighter green she'd grown accustomed to without her powers.

Long gray scars appeared on her arms as well, identical to the ones she'd seen on the elemental.

What had caused those? Had they happened when her earth power had been ripped from her?

The rest of Christine neatened up as well, her claws becoming solid, her shirt changing into a clean white tunic over a long black skirt.

Huh. Was this what royalty was supposed to wear?

Christine was *not* about to put a gold or diamond-encrusted crown on her head, though she thought about it.

Not until she could get in front of a mirror and experiment with what looked best.

Only when Christine at least appeared to be clean and fit for company did she push open the door to the courtroom.

It looked much like the first courtroom she'd been in. Directly opposite her stood a wooden dormer, set above more doors. It looked like the doors she'd just come through, dark, with fancy scrollwork. In front of the door sat a human-looking judge in formal black robes that flowed down to his wrists, with a high, Peter-pan collar.

To the left of the judge, and a step down, sat three demons in similar black robes, though the robes looked more like what Ming Dao had been wearing—looser, possibly to disguise their non-human bodies. The first demon was at least humanoid, though sickly white, with a long, noseless face and large fangs dripping down from its gaping mouth. The next was gray and scaly, like a rock come to life, with gleaming red eyes and just a black hole where its mouth should be. The third was an angry red color, with great sharp horns and an ox-like face.

They made Christine bristle. They weren't *right*. Why were they here?

To the right of the judge sat three angels, also wearing those formal black robes. They all had a human-like appearance, though the one on the far right had a face that looked like a child's. (A seraph, perhaps?) The other two were older, one African-American, one Asian. White light spilled from them.

Christine realized the light emanating from them was merely magical in nature, not Heavenly. Huh. The child angel had tiny wings that sprouted from her shoulders, while the others had great, sweeping wings that swayed gently behind them.

Most of the wooden benches that took up the rest of the room were empty. A couple of creatures—both with patchwork skin and bright white hair—sat holding hands in the very last seat.

Then Christine saw her family, sitting in the front row.

A tall human-like creature talked with them earnestly. Was that an angel? In the formal court robes?

On the other side of the aisle of benches sat Lars and his family. A demon talked with them.

Where was Tina? Christine assumed she and her family would be there soon.

Court hadn't started yet.

Christine hurried forward. Mum saw her first, started, but then rose and gave her daughter a warm hug.

"How are you?" Mum asked, leaning back but still holding Christine's arms tightly. She cocked her head to the side. "You look well. Better."

Christine couldn't help but grin. "I'm well, Mum. Whole."

That caused a ripple through the entire courtroom, as if a sudden wind had sprung up and tugged at all the robes.

Christine paused and looked around the room. Most of the beings were staring at her.

At least some of the stares appeared to be friendly.

Dad stood up and flung an arm over Christine's shoulder, giving her a hug, though she was a couple of inches taller than he was. She tried not to wince as he squeezed her hurt shoulder.

"That's swell, sweetheart!" he said enthusiastically. "Glad to hear you're better."

Christine stopped herself from rolling her eyes. Really, who said "swell" anymore?

Only her dad.

Dennis stayed seated where he was, looking sourly at her. "So I missed all the adventure," he complained.

Christine nodded. "And a good thing, too. You would have died. Tina almost did."

Dennis give her a second look. Then his eyes narrowed. "Are you okay? I bet that's an illusion you're wearing. How injured are you?"

Christine grimaced. But then she told her family the truth. "I am wearing an illusion. I'm an absolute wreck, right now." That at least gave her the excuse to remove her dad's arm from around her shoulders. "Hurt," she said gently.

"Hurt?" Mum asked, worried.

"I'm already healing," Christine assured her.

The angel who'd been speaking to her parents gave her a long, piercing look, nodding his head. "It was a smart choice to hide your appearance and your wounds. It shows respect for the court," the angel said. He cast a glance over at where Lars and his family sat.

While Mrs. and Mr. Sorgenfrey were dressed in nice enough outfits, Lars still wore his stained and dirty T-shirt and shorts.

"Mr. Kiraman was explaining the charges," Mum said.

Christine couldn't help but growl, "What charges?" What had she done wrong? She'd been the one wronged, her powers taken from her. She had never had a chance to be herself, to learn as she should have. Her heritage had been stolen from her.

"For your family, aiding and abetting the breaking of your bindings," Mr. Kiraman said.

"It was *my* choice," Christine told him. "Plus, those bindings were illegal. I'm not a criminal."

"Just because your powers might have been bound

illegally doesn't mean that breaking those bindings, without a court order, was legal," Mr. Kiraman explained. "Two wrongs don't make a right."

Christine kept her growl to herself. On the one hand, he was correct. If breaking a binding was illegal, she'd done so willfully.

On the other hand, what choice had she had?

"The additional charge, and the more serious, in my opinion, is the willful destruction of the fairy bridge," Mr. Kiraman said.

Christine bit her lips together. What he said was true—she had destroyed the bridge, even knowing what it was.

"I did promise to rebuild it," Christine told him.

Mr. Kiraman stood up straighter and gave her a beatific smile. "Did you, now?" he asked.

Christine watched, fascinated. She'd never have expected that an angelic creature could look so much like a cat with stolen cream.

Christine nodded. "Before I took back my air elemental."

"Just a moment, let me check," the angel said. His eyes grew all white and he stood as still as a statue.

Christine wasn't sure why that made all the hairs on the back of her neck stand up, why his posture made her want to flee. But she stood her ground. She was telling the truth. There wasn't anything for her to be afraid of.

She hoped.

After a long moment, the angel came back. "The promise *was* recorded," he said with wonder.

"Where?" Christine asked, curious. When she'd

spoken the words, they'd felt important. She remembered that bell-like tone ringing deep in the earth.

The angel looked at her quizzically for a moment, before he nodded. "That's right. You're a changeling. You didn't realize that when troll royalty promise something, their words are often held in the earth, so they can be held accountable at the end of their days."

Christine shook her head slowly. Wow. So her words and her promises *were* important.

Dad reached out and squeezed her hand. "It's a good thing that Tuckermans have always kept their promises."

The angel looked at Christine's dad, then her mum, in puzzlement. "How interesting," he said softly. Then he turned back to Christine. "You were placed in this family without their knowing, correct?"

Christine nodded. "Exchanged for Tina, my human doppelganger, so she could grow up with all the magical training she needed for her Destiny."

"Fascinating," the angel said. "The LORD moves in mysterious ways."

Before Christine could ask him what he meant by that, the judge rapped the gavel on the desk in front of him.

"All rise!" A wolf guard, who looked kind of how Ty did when he was half-transformed, stepped forward.

Everyone stood, even the judge and his advisors.

"Court is now in session. Preliminary arguments may begin."

CHAPTER 12

"Prophecy is a funny thing," Mr. Kiraman said as he strode back and forth at the front of the courtroom. "It's generally treated as gospel, though what the oracles predict and what occurs are frequently two different things."

Christine watched, fascinated. His ghost wings held themselves perfectly still as he was addressing the court, through what looked like concentrated effort on his part. Were they some kind of "tell"? Would they show more of his emotions than he wanted to let on, if he allowed them to just wave as they wanted to?

The judge and the two sets of the Host, the angels and the demons sitting at the front of the courtroom, watched politely as well. Christine couldn't tell if they were actually interested, or if they had already made up their minds.

No jury sat to hear the evidence. It was all to be presented before the court, the judge making the final decision as advised by the demons and angels.

Tina and her family had shown up after the first hour

or so. Tina still looked frayed, pale and shaking. At least she was no longer in those ridiculous robes, but a normal dark brown T-shirt and jeans.

Whatever had happened during that battle had really taken it out of Tina. Christine had only seen part of it, but it had seemed to her to be endless, and not just a fight about magical strength, but willpower.

Had the demons Tina been fighting real? There was a taste to them, pale and thin, that still made Christine question their reality.

The human judge (though Christine wasn't positive he was one hundred percent human—she suspected he just appeared that way) had been impressed that Christine had promised to rebuild the bridge. And no one had accused her family (just yet) of being criminals, just of not stopping Christine.

Mr. Kiraman had explained all of Christine's actions as reasonable, given the circumstances. She was a being with her powers taken against her will. She hadn't killed anyone, just damaged property. Who could blame her, really?

He was finally getting to the heart of the argument. Christine could tell by how his wings now appeared to be carved out of light, completely unwavering.

Mr. Kiraman pointed to Tina. "It's been declared for some time now that this human has a Destiny," he said. "Christine suffered under a changeling spell for decades in order to protect her human doppelganger." He paused dramatically. "But could it be that the oracles were misinterpreted? That it is Christine, instead, who has a Destiny?"

Mr. Kiraman gave another great pause. "I petition the court to unseal the records behind Christine's true heritage."

The judge nodded. "I have reviewed the records around Ms. Tuckerman's adoption." He shot a hard look at the Zimmerman's. "While it appears that the letter of the law has been followed, the spirit of it has definitely been bent."

Mr. and Mrs. Zimmerman raised their chins in defiance. Christine could already hear their excuses.

At least the court recognized that they hadn't done the right thing, regardless of the legality of it.

"However," the judge continued. "Prophecy, as you say, is a tricky thing. Particularly when dealing with *kith and kin.*" He paused. "In order to continue, I say that—"

"Your honor! Sir!"

A troll burst into the courtroom. He stood taller than Christine or Joe. He wore a long white shirt that hung down to mid-thigh, with a fancy purple plaque down the center of it, and black short-cropped pants that ended just above the knee. His dark green skin appeared unmarred, but Christine still had the impression of age. Maybe it was his yellow tusks, maybe it was his white-streaked brown hair.

The judge banged his gavel. "Bailiff, remove this being," he said.

"I have pertinent information regarding the political prisoner," the troll said hastily.

"Political prisoner?" the judge asked. He held up his hand to stall the bailiff. "Who?"

The troll pointed directly at Christine. "Her. Princess Kizalynn Linumok Te'Dur."

~

Christine sat in between Mum and Dad, simmering with barely controlled rage. The judge and his advisors were meeting in chambers with the troll who had just shown up and announced that Christine was a political prisoner.

While Christine…waited.

She should have been included in their conversations! How dare they?

Who had been holding her as a political prisoner? Had it been the demons? The Sorgenfrey's and their counsel had had some serious, huddled conversation for a while before they'd gone back to sitting and waiting.

Mum had held Christine's hand for a while. However, Christine still didn't like being touched that much, or that often, even by her family. She suffered it for a while, however, in part because Mum had seemed particularly fascinated by Christine's tough and smooth hide, the scars on her arms, the sharpness of her claws.

Mr. Kiraman had no idea what was going on, though he'd gone off to do his own investigation as well. However, he'd reappeared empty-handed, with no new information.

Princess Kizalynn Linumok Te'Dur. That was the only part that kept Christine from tearing apart the entire courtroom, as well as going *through* the bailiff, to find out what exactly that other troll had meant. She needed to talk with him. Hear what he had to say. Badger him until he told her the truth.

Christine had suspected for some time that she was royalty. Only troll royalty were magical, and she was very, *very* magical. She knew that, particularly now that she had her powers back.

The powers within her couldn't offer any help, beyond the image that her air power had already shown her—of an old troll king sitting alone on his throne. The image carried the sadness the troll felt. He had no heirs, no kin. Christine didn't know how she knew that, just that she did.

Was that Christine's bio-dad? He didn't look anything like her. Or like her earth power. His face was much flatter and broader than Christine's or Joe's. Silver caps topped the huge tusks that grew up from the king's powerful jaw. He kept his hair cropped short, maybe a quarter inch of bristling gray covering his head.

Like the outfit that Christine's earth power had chosen for her, the king wore a long white tunic over plain black pants that chopped off just below the knee. However, his shirt was made from some gorgeous linen, with cream-colored embroidery along the front plaque, cuffs, and collar.

He was the same shade of green as her earth power—a little darker than her natural coloring. And his arms, legs, and probably chest and back, held gray scars from wounds that hadn't healed completely.

How were they related? Why was he important? Why was he all alone?

Christine had far too many questions, and everyone who might answer them was behind locked doors.

So she waited. And she didn't growl. Much.

Finally, the bailiff came out of the chambers behind the courtroom. "All rise!" he commanded.

Christine shot to her feet. Finally! They were getting somewhere.

The judge and his advisors came out. After they sat, the rest of the courtroom did as well.

Where was the other troll? Why hadn't he come back as well?

Christine wasn't sure how she would find him, but she would hunt him through the entire city. Hell, to Trollville and back, to get her answers.

"In light of the new evidence placed before me, I say we have serious charges involving kidnapping and imprisonment to investigate," the judge said, staring hard at the Zimmermans.

Christine couldn't help her smug satisfaction. She knew she wasn't a good person for wanting the Zimmermans to face some sort of punishment for the way they'd treated her, adopting her just so they could use her as a changeling.

But still…they were Tina's parents. And she was as innocent as Christine. It would be tough on Tina if her parents were convicted of something.

"Your honor?" Christine asked in the shocked silence of the courtroom.

Mr. Kiraman turned and shook his head at Christine.

She stubbornly stood up and continued.

"Is there the possibility of demonic influence on the

Zimmermans? I certainly have seen evidence of that, with Tina."

The judge narrowed his eyes at the Zimmermans, then shot another hard look at the Sorgenfreys. "Free will is a sovereign right by decree of the LORD," he said. "I command that all demonic influence over these humans cease and desist immediately!"

"And my parents, too," Christine piped up.

"All the humans in this courtroom," the judge growled.

Mr. and Mrs. Sorgenfrey glanced at each other, then shrugged in unison.

Seemed they had no choice.

The sickly yellow light that bled off of Christine's mum and dad, as well as Dennis, was pale in comparison to the one that the Zimmermans shed. All three of them.

Huh. Christine had just wanted to make sure that Tina was going to be okay. She hadn't imagined her parents might have been influenced.

"Your binding and sentencing will be carried out in a separate hearing," the judge declared, indicating the Sorgenfreys.

"But your honor—" started their demon attorney.

"Now," the judge growled. He banged his gavel. They all disappeared in a puff of smoke.

Christine didn't know if that was good or bad, if Lars and his family would be able to wriggle out of their bindings again.

It didn't matter. She would be more than ready for him, practicing with all her powers daily. Integrating them.

"If I might continue?" the judge asked sarcastically. He stared at Christine.

"Sorry," Christine said, sitting quickly.

"We have heard the case from Mr. Kiraman," the judge continued. "We have the physical evidence entered into evidence. We have the private testimony of Ming Dao."

Christine bristled at that. Shouldn't his part in all of this be made public? He had claimed to be part of a secret order, working against the other demons. Maybe they'd had to take his testimony privately in order to keep him alive, like some kind of witness protection for demons.

"And we have other evidence from Hamin Shaenez Kunza, the herald from the court in Trollville," the judge said.

Christine couldn't *wait* to talk with him.

The judge addressed Christine directly. "It appears that you were taken, and hidden, here in the human realm, against the wishes of your family."

Christine nodded and blinked back sudden tears. She *knew* she'd been stolen. Her bio-parents hadn't wanted to give her up.

"However, the perpetrators of the act also have a prophecy to back up their actions. They believe that if you'd remained in the court, you would have been killed, and rather quickly." The judge paused. "I'm to understand that the scars you bear on your arms are the result of the first assassination attempt, when you were barely a year old."

Christine looked down at her arms. Someone had tried to kill her as a baby? They'd hurt her badly, too.

She looked back up at the judge and shrugged. She didn't remember.

The judge nodded. "However, there are still your crimes to consider."

Christine tamped down on her anger. She'd been kidnapped as a baby, her powers ripped from her and stolen away. She didn't owe anyone anything at this point.

"The destruction of the fairy bridge is a terrible crime against all *kith and kin*," the judge said sternly. "Cutting off the families here from their loved ones in their worlds. Making all the worlds more vulnerable to attack as they relax the strictures against portals."

Christine pressed her lips together. She knew she'd have to pay for that. But what did the judge want?

"Since you've already promised to rebuild the bridge, I hereby order you to be held to that promise before you continue onto Trollville, to take your rightful place," the judge proclaimed, rapping his gavel on his desk. "In addition, your parents here will help."

He didn't look at Mum or Dad. He stared, instead, at the Zimmermans.

Christine nearly snickered. They were, on paper, her adoptive parents.

The Tuckermans had merely believed she was their daughter, and had just raised her as such.

Legally, however, they had no relationship to Christine.

"We'll help as well," Mum said clearly into the quiet following the judge's orders.

The judge turned and beamed at them.

He really wasn't human. There was probably both

angelic and demonic blood in him, Christine finally decided. A mix of both that hopefully made him more neutral.

"I was hoping you'd say that. It will give both families the opportunity to get to know each other better. And for Christine's adoptive parents to actually learn about their daughter," he said.

The judge banged his gavel one last time on his desk, the crack sounding like the lightning before a big thunderstorm.

"This court is dismissed."

Christine kept trying to remember to close her mouth as Hamin Shaenez Kunza, the herald from the court at Trollville, told her about her history.

They sat in a small café on the first floor of the courthouse. Behind Christine, the traffic on Fourth moved at a crawled. Seemed there was the usual construction just up the street. It was a Sunday, so not as many pedestrians walked along the sidewalk.

Hamin had insisted that they meet in a public place to talk, though Christine had no idea why. However, once they'd gotten their drinks and were seated, he cupped his hand and deliberately circled them, so that no other creature could make out what they were saying.

"Your uncle, actually, is the king," Hamin told her. "You're the daughter of the king's younger brother."

"So I'm not a princess?" Christine asked, trying to hide her disappointment.

"You are royalty," Hamin said. "And since all of the king's children have either died or been killed, you were in line for the throne. You had been officially declared an heir. You are royalty. The technical term is princess, as you're in line for being queen."

Queen. Christine kind of liked the sound of that. She'd used magic to view herself wearing various tiaras the night before while looking in the mirror. None of them had looked right, or regal enough.

Maybe it was because her only references were human crowns. She was going to have to try it again, only this time, decorate the tiara with the jewels that most appealed to a troll, those uncut gems she'd seen in her daydreams.

Christine remembered the sad old troll king, all alone on his throne. "Who was behind the deaths of all of the king's heirs?" she asked.

Hamin shrugged. "Some were accidental. We think. But others… No one knows for certain, m'Lady."

Christine almost snorted at that. Her. A lady.

Yeah, right.

"When you disappeared, suspicion fell on your father, the grand duke. He's been wasting away in prison ever since."

Christine shook her head. "I bet he was the one who saved me from the first attempt, wasn't he?" she asked.

Hamin tilted his head to one side. "How did you know that?" he said. "He was the one who rescued you from the Ork Flame. It's the only fire that will damage a troll, and burns forever."

Christine shivered. She looked down at her arms. She wasn't showing her scars today, but she felt them, sometimes. Like the previous night, when she'd tried to sleep. They'd pulsed at her. Not aching, but wanting…something.

When she laid her hands over them, she realized the long scars formed patterns. Like handprints.

Were they the prints of the person who'd thrown her into the Ork Flame? Or were they of the person who'd tried to pull her out of it?

"You must return to Trollville," Hamin said urgently. "You need to claim your throne. And to help your father. If he's innocent, he shouldn't spend another day in jail."

Christine opened her mouth, then shut it again. "I promised to stay here and rebuild the bridge, first. Then I will come. Nothing will be able to stop me."

Hamin shook his head. "They will find something else. Some other cause that will delay you." He sighed. "They've been clever, our enemies. Far too clever. And we are merely trolls."

"I *will* come," Christine insisted, "once I finish the bridge. I pro—"

"Don't, m'Lady," Hamin said, interrupting her. "I would not have you forsworn."

"I will come," she promised him anyway.

"I know you'll try," Hamin said. But he refused to believe her, refused to be consoled.

"You know, Mum and Dad always treated you like a princess," Dennis said sourly. "Spoiled you rotten."

Christine *very gently* thwacked her brother on the shoulder as they walked. They'd found parking in the lot just outside the Japanese Garden at the Arboretum and were now walking toward where the bridge had once stood.

"Ow!" he complained, rubbing his shoulder.

"That didn't hurt," Christine told him.

They paused for another car to pass before they could cross the street. It was mid-afternoon on a Saturday. They were going to meet Mum and Dad, as well as Tina and Mr. and Mrs. Zimmerman for a picnic, to discuss their plans for the bridge. Bright sunlight shone down through the trees, dappling the hot pavement.

"Did too hurt," Dennis said.

Christine opened her mouth, then closed it again. She wouldn't be drawn into a squabble with her brother, not even one that wasn't serious, given the grin he then gave her.

She'd spent too many hours with her own powers squabbling inside of her. She couldn't stand to listen to more arguing. Though her elementals didn't argue as much as they had initially, they still frequently disturbed her peace.

It had only been a week since the court had given its declaration. Christine wished the families could have met earlier, but everyone else had work.

Christine had a job as well, at the library, though she was thinking about giving notice once she'd started doing real work on the bridge. Or at least taking a sabbatical, if the library would let her.

She had to finish the bridge. And soon. Hamin had left her unsettled.

"You know, I *do* think it's kinda cool that you're royalty, right?" Dennis asked as they started up the regular path.

"Really?" Christine asked. "Why's that?"

"You're probably rich, right?" Dennis said reasonably.

Christine held up her hand, threatening to thwack him again.

Dennis flinched. "Kidding!" he said, admitting defeat. "But seriously, Sis. I told you not to let it go to your head. And it hasn't," he said hastily when she might have growled at him.

"It's…It's a big change, though," he continued after a moment.

"I know," Christine said. "But you're still my brother."

He was the only family she'd ever known. Even if they weren't actually related.

"That I am," Dennis said proudly. "You might want to make sure to tell Mum and Dad something like that too. And often."

"I will," Christine told him fervently. "I promise."

The ringing tones that generally accompanied those words didn't sound that time. It wasn't a promise of trollish royalty.

It didn't matter. Christine took it just as seriously.

Mum and Dad were still her family. And though they were human, they mattered.

Dennis and Christine crested the hill. On the far side, near the broken rocks, stood the Zimmermans, looking at the damage. Dad was obviously trying to talk with them, though they were ignoring him.

Probably failing to tell a joke, as always.

Mum stood quietly by herself, her arms crossed over her chest, looking sad.

Christine understood. She hated the damage she saw, the broken stones.

But she'd fix them. Make them better than they'd been. Reopen the path to the lands of *kith and kin*.

And then finally walk that path herself, all the way to Trollville.

Dennis gave a low whistle. "You're going to fix that?" he asked.

"I have to. I promised," Christine told him.

Dennis nodded. "Then let's get started."

Christine followed him down the hill. He was right. It was time to get started.

"Hey," Christine called as she walked through the portal into Nikolai's shop. The shop was empty of customers. Just Nikolai stood behind the counter at the front.

The powers inside Christine started, or at least that was what it felt like. As though they'd all been resting and jumped slightly.

But none of them demanded her immediate attention. They were still integrating. She was still learning how to work with all of her elementals.

There was so much she wanted to learn about her powers. However, there was also only so much she could do on her own. She was a magical creature, yes, but magic also had structure.

She needed help, though she wasn't as helpless as she'd once been.

Nikolai stirred where he was standing. It seemed to Christine that he'd been sleeping on his feet, no animation in his face or features.

Then he came to life abruptly.

"Hello, Christine," Nikolai said. Then he gave her a huge smile, his lips moving but not. "Or should I say, 'your highness.'"

Christine couldn't help but roll her eyes at him. "That isn't necessary," she said in a prissy voice, teasing him back.

Nikolai gave her a snorting laugh, then asked, "What can I do for you?"

Christine sighed. "I still need your help learning magic." She didn't know who else to go to. While Tina was willing to help teach her, Christine now believed Nikolai's warning that she shouldn't trust a human.

Even her family had all been under demonic influence.

"You know I've never worked with troll royalty, before," Nikolai said. "I can make guesses about your magic, and try to direct your studies, but you need a better Merlin."

Christine nodded, relieved. At least Nikolai admitted that he didn't know everything. "I think between us we'll be able to figure it out," she said. "You'll be a fine Merlin."

"As long as you don't expect me to get younger," Nikolai said. He shuddered. "I'd never want to go back to being a teenager."

Christine didn't know how to reply to that. Nikolai was a made man, right? He'd never had to grow up, or go through the agony of hormones and acne.

Had he?

Christine would have to remember to ask later if he was just teasing or not.

"I just need your help," Christine said quietly. "How to use my powers—I've got a handle on that. But I have no idea how to cast spells, or do formal magic."

Nikolai nodded and looked thoughtful. "So, you want to continue with your magic lessons?" he asked.

"Yes, please," Christine said relieved. She hadn't thought that Nikolai would deny her, but she hadn't been absolutely certain.

"I do have these old books that need cataloging," Nikolai said slowly.

Christine nodded. "I can help with that." She wasn't

certain when she'd have the time—rebuilding the bridge was going to eat up every spare minute she had.

However, she also knew she had to be prepared.

There would be more battles. Magical and physical. She was going to have to know how to defend herself.

And her kingdom.

"Then let's begin, shall we, highness?" Nikolai asked. He held open the drapery that covered the door to the back room.

"I thank ye, sir," Christine said regally as she passed before him, eager to start the next part of her life.

ABOUT THE AUTHOR

Leah Cutter writes page-turning fiction in exotic locations, such as a magical New Orleans, the ancient Orient, Hungary, the Oregon coast, rural Kentucky, Seattle, Minneapolis, and many others.

She writes literary, fantasy, mystery, science fiction, and horror fiction. Her short fiction has been published in magazines like *Alfred Hitchcock's Mystery Magazine* and *Talebones*, anthologies like Fiction River, and on the web. Her long fiction has been published both by New York publishers as well as small presses.

Find Leah's books here.

Follow her blog at www.LeahCutter.com.

Reviews

It's true. Reviews help me sell more books. If you've enjoyed this story, please consider leaving a review of it on your favorite site.

Come someplace new…

Are you a traveler? Do you enjoy exploring strange new worlds, new cultures, new people?

Sign up for my newsletter and I'll start you on your travels with a free copy of my book, *The Island Sampler*.

I will never spam you or use your email for nefarious purposes. You can also unsubscribe at any time.

http://www.LeahCutter.com/newsletter/

ABOUT KNOTTED ROAD PRESS

Knotted Road Press fiction specializes in dynamic writing set in mysterious, exotic locations.

Knotted Road Press non-fiction publishes autobiographies, business books, cookbooks, and how-to books with unique voices.

Knotted Road Press creates DRM-free ebooks as well as high-quality print books for readers around the world.

With authors in a variety of genres including literary, poetry, mystery, fantasy, and science fiction, Knotted Road Press has something for everyone.

Knotted Road Press
www.KnottedRoadPress.com

www.ingramcontent.com/pod-product-compliance
Lightning Source LLC
Chambersburg PA
CBHW070640100726
47907CB00007B/2051